Wight Dia

& Crazy Red

Dogs

Glynis.M.Parkes

Glynis.M.Parkes

ISBN: 9798773876465

CONTENTS

Glynis M Parkes first in the series novel Chale Hath No Fury was released in early 2021, Wight Diamonds & Crazy Red Dogs is the 2nd book in the Isle of Wight Crime Thriller series.

Also by this Author: **End of May 1923** – debut novel based on a true story of talented sportsman Fred & his wife Sarah Parkes, who lived in a small Staffordshire mining village. Starting with the WW1 years, this love story takes you back to a different era, Fred was a hero, he loved football and his local cricket club in Pelsall, Staffordshire. Sarah had a dream, but would he listen? A shocking heart wrenching outcome that would change lives forever. Family secrets buried in a deafening silence for 100 years …

All available on Amazon/Kindle – paperback or ebook

ACKNOWLEDGMENTS

Coming out of the 2020 pandemic means back to normality, but will life ever be the same? It's a good time to read and take yourself off to those places you love. The Isle of Wight is our place...

Thank you to my family and endless packets of biscuits for their support.

CHAPTER 1

Maria stared at her visitor through the thick glass screen that had finger marks all over it. Those smudges irritated her tidy organised mind, as she fidgeted restlessly on the stool that was too low for dignity or comfort, making her feel inferior to the occupant of the taller chair opposite on the other side of the filthy glass.

She could only just see the right hand edge of the tall black metal chair surrounding the body of her visitor; but she could hear, very clearly, a hideous distracting squeak every time he moved which made her flinch. It would have been quite funny to anyone else, but Maria was a humourless woman so the morsel of remaining humour, after ten years in this cold suffocating place, was paper thin because it made him look considerably superior at that moment. That squeaking chair was doing nothing to improve her rapidly increasing agitation.

Even before the prison sentence Maria Hayward found very little joy in anything. She was a serious, matter of fact, blustery woman who liked things done to a high standard. Did they provide tall squeaking chairs on purpose to feed the humiliation in here? She wanted and felt she deserved to be, at least, on the same level as him and for some indescribable reason fuelling the irritation, she wanted a cloth in her hand to polish the glass until it shone. There was very little else to concentrate the mind in here except her new visitor and the finger marks that filled her eyes and brain; they appeared to be taunting her. In ten years, he was the only other person, apart from her solicitor, that she had allowed to visit her in this place so why had she permitted the visit now? Her curiosity had got the better of her. What did he want?

Devlin Marshall, stared back at her with a look that simmered making him difficult to analyse. What was he thinking? Is that a look that could kill? Or was it sympathy? She could not tell, after all this time her grip on reality had been watered down to just an impartial trickle. She had learned that a kind look in here usually meant the opposite, so she was suspicious of every glance, every approach, and even the slightest trace of emotion made her withdraw even further into her own head. Getting something for nothing in prison was not an option.

He was still as handsome as she remembered which made her feel even more awkward and uncomfortable. He looked fresh, tanned and alive, so different to the prisoners and warders in here who lumbered around, shoulders drooping, with skin pallor like death masks. Ten years inside the prison had done nothing for her own looks or her manner. In the outside world Maria had been proud of the way she looked and dressed, some said overdressed, for any occasion. Full make-up every day with matching shoes and handbag with plenty of jewellery the norm every day. There was nothing casual or dull about the way Maria Hayward presented herself to the world back then. But now... prison issue grey, a bar of soap and a rough textured towel were her world. Pride had gone out of the window and survival every day, top of the agenda, replacing real 'things' of which she had nothing left after the fire that burned her house to the ground ten years ago in 1969.

Of course she had thought about him, probably every day since he disappeared after the Chale Bay Operation when he vanished off the face of the earth. She had wanted a relationship with him and had offered it, along with a place on her team; to be by her side in the Organisation. And what had he done? Left her high and dry to deal with death and the aftermath without an explanatory word. He just disappeared; now here he was, bold as brass, bloody cheek.

In truth he was feeling as nervous as she was and knew he had to play this carefully to get her onside after what he had done; informing the police about the drugs and guns, brought in by tanker, off-loaded into small boats in Chale Bay and stashed in a cave on the beach. They should have been distributed around the country and the world, but it ended in failure because of him. He ended Maria's dream of wealth beyond her wildest dreams. Thankfully, she knew nothing of what he did, but maybe she put two and two together. There were plenty of people involved who could have blown the Operation, he just felt she might know it was him, that was his guilt. The next 15 minutes were crucial.

She had high hopes for them both back then, a professional relationship for sure, a personal relationship? Maybe... but he had been as cold as a fish. In her head she suspected it was him who had given the game away that day leading to the swoop on the beach and the goods being confiscated by the authorities. All those police on the beach grabbing the drugs and guns out of the cave. Goods brought in by tanker from South America, she had hoped it would be the last time after many successful smaller cargo's, the one in 1969 was the biggest haul ever and it should have made her a very rich woman. It could have been so different. The anger and the 'what if's' had been fading as the years melted away, but this visit was bringing it all back and she sat there seething at the sight of him.

"Maria," one word and it cut her like a knife.

"What the hell do you want?" she spat out the question.

"That's not very nice is it? I thought you would be pleased to see a friendly face. I gather nobody bothers to come and see you," he grinned and waited.

She said nothing for a few minutes, but he could see the cogs whirring inside her head. It was in her eyes, they were dancing in the bright florescent lights overhead. No escape in this concentrated, crushing, environment.

"Nice? NICE? Who the hell do you think you are coming here and being smarmy with me? I know it was you, so don't even try to deny it," she stared at him with the fierce intense glare of an enemy. She slammed her hand flat on the glass in an angry gesture that clearly indicated, 'if this glass wasn't here I would shoot you too.' Her face was evil, and he noticed. Had he blown it already?

Time inside this grey and depressing place had not softened her demeaner; if anything she had hardened and learned quickly that this was no place for being soft. She was serving life for killing her business partner Matt Hayward. She shot him. One bullet in the neck after he tried to burn her alive in her own house. They could not prove she was involved in the drugs and arms heist in Chale Bay in 1969, she was too clever and had covered her tracks. The fire destroyed any evidence that might have incriminated her, and probably would have increased her sentence, but there were too many witnesses to the shooting so here she had been for the last ten years. She was hopeful her sentence could be just another five years or less and then she would be back. Planning in her head before she went to sleep each night, on that hard striped prison issue pillow, how she could get her life back. Her brain functioned but she kept the thoughts and the hopes hidden inside the false blank shell her face portrayed to anybody who looked in her direction. She gave nothing away to anybody and concentrated on just getting by from day to day in the hell hole she called her current miserable home.

Devlin Marshall had sent a visiting order to Blaydorn prison again, probably the eighth in as many years, in the hope that she would see him, and he was more than surprised when that request to see her was finally granted. He had not finished with Maria Hayward just yet. He suspected she had taken the vast stash of money, and whatever else was in the boxes, from Matts bank vault in Zurich during the planning of the heist and was sitting quite literally on a fortune, ready for when she got released.

Matt Hayward, Maria's business partner for a decade before Devlin met her was shot, by Maria in the Old Mill House. That assassination left a hundred unanswered questions. Where was the money Matt had creamed off the business, duping suppliers and

Cartels then put into a vault in Zurich? He played a dangerous game, so did he pay with his life? Everybody in the Paris office knew what Matt was doing despite his denial. Putting two and two together Maria must have taken the money, otherwise why would Matt try to kill her? Devlin suspected that must be the story and he needed to find out. All of his investigations had hit a brick wall because Maria trusted and told no-one what she was up to, ever; and he needed to hear it from her, the horse's mouth, if he could gain her trust.

"You are looking well considering Maria," he gushed and gulped at the lie.

"Was it you?" She ignored the compliment going straight for the burning question.

"Was it me what?" He asked as innocently as his face would allow.

"Who blew the Operation. I don't know why I am asking because I know it was you, who else could it have been?" Her manner was flat and long rehearsed in her head. Ten years is a long time to sit and think, between changing her sheets and watching episodes of Crossroads on a 12inch black and white television. She had done very little else in there, flower arranging, and jigsaw puzzles were just not her cup of tea.

"I got out because I had no choice, most people on the job ran that night, so I am not sure I know what you are talking about. Why would I blow the Operation? I walked away with nothing but my freedom," he lied. "I saw them coming and I ran like the others," he lied again.

Since his escape from the beach, in 1969 with part of the Class A drugs haul in a big black bag, he had kept his head down.   He probably salvaged more out of the Chale Bay heist than any of them.

Knowing Maria had killed the love of his life, Martyn Squire, on the boat in Cowes, that firework night in August 1969 he wanted revenge on her and indeed he had blown the whole thing that night in August 1969, the weekend of the Isle of Wight Music Festival, leading to the whole Operation being discovered and blown apart.

Wanting to get rid of Matt because he got greedy and careless, Maria had ordered a hit on him and expected her staff in Paris to put a bullet in his head, a quick end! But the people she trusted to do the deed had taken their own initiative and placed explosives on a boat in Cowes bay on fireworks night 1969.   Martyn Squire was on board, and he was blown to pieces by the explosion. Matt Hayward and Devlin Marshall failed to board the boat that night and lived to realise it was probably Maria who was responsible wanting them all dead.

There was a huge question mark of doubt over who had betrayed them, but she felt sure that it was Devlin. Call it a gut feeling, feminine intuition. Somebody informed the police that night, -if it wasn't him, why did he disappear? He intended for that piece of information to stay well-hidden for the foreseeable future, it not forever.

Her head was back in 1969, asking him to be part of her life both professionally and personally.   He would keep denying his involvement that led to the failure of the Operation and keep up that pretence for his own preservation. It was like a game to both of them, for now. It could have been any of the 20 odd crew, she would never find out for certain that it was him.

"I read some bits about your case, but I was abroad, so it was difficult to get the whole story, to this day I don't know why you did what you did, why Matt? I thought you and he were rock solid. I have to admit Maria I was shocked when I heard. What did he do to you, did he have an affair or a fight over money? Usually one of those factors ends a relationship," he waited and watched more cogs whirring in her head, reflected in the movement in her eyes and body language.

He had memory of some conversations with Matt and clearly remembered him saying he was getting out soon, that he had to look after himself, but he never said why or what he really meant. If he did say then it was long forgotten. It had to be either their relationship or the Organisation or both? He would never know now, he should have been a better listener. He also got the feeling that whatever relationship Matt had with Maria was long over and there was someone else in his life.

Devlin suspected it was Jess, the woman that he met at Maria's once, but it was only a suspicion, and he hadn't seen or heard from her for a decade. Maybe she might have some answers. He made a mental note to see if she still lived next door to The Copse. Maria and Matt had few friends, but she seemed to be ensconced in their small circle so worth a shot if she still lived next door in the Old Mill House.

Maria could not work out why he was there. Where had he been for ten years and why now? She had vague memories of somebody wanting to visit her in the past, maybe it was him she couldn't remember. She shut herself off when she entered those walls, vowing to block out anything from her past, the last ten years had dissolved into a murky fog in her head. Why was he interested in her? She could not say for certain whether or not he had been involved with the Operations failure, but she was no fool. It was not easy, blocking it all out, years of festering thoughts had made her angry at times when she had allowed herself to remember what happened. But recently her brain had swung back into gear after hearing about a Parole appeal being granted and up for a decision in the next few weeks; he was top of her list for revenge, if ever she got out of here and the opportunity arose.

Strangely she missed Matt. Her partner for ten years, just a business partner but they had pretended to be married to give the illusion of strength and trust to their illegal dealings with Cartels and drug barons all over the world. They had so many secrets between them, it acted like strong glue bonding them together. Towards the end she found out he was keeping too many things to himself, and she could not accept that, but if she could undo what she did then that would happen in a heartbeat, but no point dwelling.

There was no love match, ever, but a desire to make money and a strange mutual respect, both being in awe of the other when it came to being daring and unafraid of taking risks.

But that was in the beginning, and it led to the necessity to be together to fuel the business. They worked well together, supporting each other but there was not much mutual respect in the end, just suspicion and hatred and jealousy born out of a power struggle between them and probably the need for love that had been absent for her, except for casual flings over the years, she had no family, few friends and little real love in her life.

Maria shot Matt in a revenge fury after escaping from her own burning house. Set by Matt, who thought she had emptied his boxes of money that he had squirrelled away in a bank vault in Zurich. He grabbed her and threw her into the secret wing of the house, hidden behind the bookcase in the hallway of The Copse, locked the door and laced the building with petrol, set fire to it and left her to perish.

Miraculously she got out and followed him, killing him with one shot from a handgun. Fired in a neighbour's house – The Old Mill House, where he had gone to lure Jess Norton to go away with him.

Jess! Now that was a shock. Matt and Jess! She had no idea about those two, but apparently it had been going on for five years. They hid it for five years! How could she have missed it? Jess was her friend, a friend to both of them.

Jess had ended it, but he never accepted it and blindly imagined she would rekindle a five year relationship with him, and they would both escape with the proceeds of years of crime. But Jess had moved on in a new relationship with Alex McFarlane and stood her ground, refusing to go with Matt who in his delusion threatened Jess with a gun in her own home. The rest as they say is history, Maria went to prison and was serving her sentence.

Maria had years to think about why Matt would try to kill her in the fire, and the only reason she came up with was the money or maybe he knew about her being responsible for ordering the explosion on the boat. Matt certainly blamed her for the money going missing from the Zurich strong boxes and Swiss Bank Account and he had his suspicions about the boat, but there had been no admissions from Maria and conversations about the money were reduced to sarcastic comments from him... but then he was never direct, always skirting around issues. Useless. That is how she remembered him, but maybe she could have dealt with it in a different way. 'Keep your friends close and your enemies closer'... something she lived by, but not when it came to Matt, how she regretted that now.

Ironically, it was not Maria who had fooled Matt.

Matt went to the Bank in Zurich to empty the strong boxes of the huge stash of money, only to find someone had been there before him. The boxes were empty, and he suspected Maria was to blame. But he was wrong. Maria took some of the money out of the bank account but didn't touch the strong boxes in the vault in Zurich, because she had not been quick enough to find the passwords or the second key that would have opened the boxes in the vault.

Alex McFarlane had the ultimate revenge on both of them and cleared the account and emptied the boxes.

Years before the Chale Bay heist, and years before he met Jess, he had been married to Suzy, a pretty, clever and vibrant woman, mother to Daisy their daughter. They needed extra money for a bigger house and a better life so in 1962, Suzy went to work for Matt and Maria Hayward, tempted by the generous pay. It supplemented her job at the University and that is where they found her in the languages department; she was naturally gifted in so many languages. Matt and Maria Hayward needed someone to help them translate documents and help them negotiate with the people they were doing illegal business with, in person and on the phone.

What they didn't tell her was that a huge section of their procurement business was dealing in illegal drugs and arms, people trafficking and false passports. Unwittingly Suzy got involved and was caught up in a business that resulted in a shocking ending for her and tragic consequences for Alex and their daughter Daisy.

Realising what she was involved in and unable to escape, she made copious notes and photographed documents that she passed on to her husband Alex. Knowing it might be useful as insurance later she even took an impression of the key to the strong boxes in Zurich. Matt was careless with his paperwork and Suzy made a note of account numbers of bank accounts That vital key that Alex used later to steal the vast amount of money right under the noses of Matt and Maria.

That last tragic day, Suzy rang Alex to say she was sorry but needed to go to Cowes with the Haywards to meet a client, so would be a bit late home, but it was their last conversation. A witness had seen a man and two women in Matts car driving at breakneck speed through the lanes on the island. They were all on their way to meet a contact, who had travelled to the Isle of Wight from South America to seal a huge deal. The car crashed into a ditch, and they left Suzy in the wreckage. Matt and Maria just walked away after dragging Suzy into the driving seat; leaving her to die and take the blame.

Taking the money from the Hayward's was the ultimate revenge for Alex following the car accident that devastated his life. Without telling a soul, Alex flew to Zurich and used the key and passwords obtained by his wife and emptied the boxes of all the money and its contents, getting back through France and crossing the Channel, calling in a favour from a contact to help him evade Customs, then hiding the proceeds in a secret safe inside the Old Mill House.

Jess who owned the Old Mill House, his girlfriend at the time, was unaware of the existence of the safe, and ten years later still had no idea of its existence hidden behind a panel in the living room.

Alex slowly and methodically laundered the money into property and assets until it was safely spread around banks and property, even into Jess's business, until it was all dispersed, all those high value notes spent. He knew that he had to act fast as decimalisation was coming in during February 1971. Jess was oblivious to all of it, she asked no questions when he put money into her business and bought the apartment for Daisy. Her naivety let her believe he earned the money from his high powered job and that is how it was left for ten years.

Maria felt it was only a matter of time before the people she had been dealing with, the Cartels and drug lords Matt had ripped off caught up with her, constantly looking over her shoulder even in that prison in case the wrong person was behind her. Maybe she would be lucky. Maybe nobody will come for her. Only time would tell.

"When do you think you will get out?" asked Devlin. A simple question but one that threw Maria.

"Why do you want to know? And why are you here? I would have thought this is the last place you would show your face. Don't try and tell me you know nothing of what happened. It had to be you. Matt was too thick to do that, he would have come off worse. I can only imagine it was you or that Alex McFarlane. But then I can't see how he would be involved in stealing my money.

"Alex McFarlane? Was that the chap who lived next door to you at The Copse?" He had heard of Alex but never met him. Devlin was wanted and Alex McFarlane and his team, working alongside Interpol were, even now, investigating crimes they believe he had committed, mainly massive jewellery thefts from Stately Homes and Museums in England, France and Russia.

"That's him. Rat. If I ever get my hands on him. If Matt hadn't been there that night it would have been him I finished off," she drifted off and looked around the room. Looking for cameras and realising she was saying too much.

"I don't know about McFarlane, but it wasn't me. I just kept my head down abroad. Got myself set up in Spain, he wasn't going to be specific, bit of windsurfing and teaching the holiday crowd a few skills but I am bored now and thought I would look you up," he waited for her to react, but she said nothing, so he continued.

"What about the house? I read bits about the fire and the trial, but I was abroad so only got some of it. Sorry to hear you went through that. Must have been a shock. What happened ?" he asked but didn't expect the reply. Maria had not spoken of the events that night, except in the courtroom when she had no choice and used the experience to plead mitigating circumstances.

"It was so quick, one minute I was drinking wine and just going to bed, I didn't turn the light on in the hall, so it was dark, next thing somebody grabbed me by the hair and threw me into the secret wing of the house and locked the door," her voice faded, and she looked at the floor as if in shock reliving the moment she had to fight for her life in that burning building.

"He set the place on fire with petrol, I could smell it, but there were keys inside the door of the hidden wing in the hall, he must have forgotten that... somehow I got out. It was black and I was choking but I wasn't going to die because of him, I knew it was him," she paused.

"How do you know it was him if it was dark?" Devlin was genuinely curious.

"He had a way of grunting when he was agitated and as he grabbed me from behind, I could hear him with that disgusting noise coming from his filthy mouth, I knew it was him, so I went after him and ended up in here. My brief tried everything to get me off and they gave me a shorter sentence because of what happened, I wasn't thinking straight, but I am still here. Hopefully for not too much longer. I have an appeal coming up in a few weeks, then I am out of here," she sounded confident and sat up straighter on the uncomfortable stool as if the realisation that freedom was a possibility.

Seeing him again gave her some hope that he might stay on if she could persuade him when she got out. The game continued, who was fooling who here? Years on her own, leading a lonely existence, had decreased her radar sensitivity on the man front. Was he interested in her? Who could say and who was he anyway? She had no more idea now than she did ten years ago. It was the first time for a very long time that she had given his background a second thought. She needed to find out more.

She was attracted to him the first time she met him. Matt found him in France, he was with Martin Squire on holiday, apparently they met in a café in Paris. Something about a museum tour. Apart from this small snippet of memory, the fog descended, and she was stuck for memory or ideas. Matt did that – just 'found' people, it was a natural talent he had. People liked him and trusted him, as had she. He didn't always get it right but reminded herself, that despite his faults, she missed Matt.

Devlin was involved with the training of the crew that took the goods off the beach, he could handle himself but how did he know all of that stuff? She couldn't even remember if she did know his background. Military she thought. Suspecting her memory may not be sparking on all its plugs she settled herself with the feeling that he bothered to come and see her and no other bu*ger had, so there must be something... right?

CHAPTER 2

Ten years before … 1969

Devlin Marshall arrived in London on August 31st, 1969, the day after the tanker arrived in Chale Bay with the massive cargo of drugs and guns.

Near to midnight on Saturday 30th August 1969 he supervised the highly trained crew while they off-loaded the haul and stashed it safely in a natural cave on a secluded headland on the south side of the Isle of Wight, South Wight.

Just after midnight he left the Isle of Wight beach at Chale Bay with a bag full of drugs, taken from the drop from the giant Oil Tanker that was sitting just out in the Bay, the boxes and wraps of drugs taken off by the crew, trained by him, sailing on small boats and carried back to the beach then stashed in the cave.

As the haul was put into the cave by this slick, silent crew in the pitch dark, without being seen by a soul, he cleverly deposited enough of the wraps of Class A drugs into his own bag.

He slipped away when the moon went behind a cloud, perfect timing, skilfully speeding across the Solent in one of three motorboats they had on standby in case of trouble, he landed on a deserted beach in Southsea. After changing his clothes he rang the police from a phone box near to Clarence Pier to inform them that the drugs and arms heist was happening on Chale beach so if they were quick could catch the culprits in the act.

He boarded the train to London, selling the drugs for a very nice sum and arranged a flight to Mallorca with the money safely deposited in a bank account set up under a false name; enough to keep him in semi-luxury for the next few years if he was careful.

Arriving in the Old Town in Palma he booked into a large hotel thinking that the bigger the hotel the more anonymous he would be, then, a few days later found a rooftop apartment with views overlooking the sparkling blue waters of the Mediterranean. The apartment was tucked inside one of the many narrow streets in the Old Town where he found it easy to melt into the cobbled maze of streets mingling with the locals, making friends easily, with both English and Spanish locals and visitors. Life was based around the myriad of local bars and cafés buried in the tall stone walls and narrow streets of the Old Town.

He set up his beach business with somebody he met in one of those tiny cafés … a 20 year old young man called Dominic Montpelier who, despite his French sounding name was in fact born on the island of Mallorca. The son of an aristocrat, François Montpelier, whose own father was from Paris, related to the Spanish Royal family on his mother's side, the family lived in some style in a vast modernised castle not too far from the harbour. The attraction for both of them was instant, like magnets attracted from a distance they came together and stayed together in a complicated and volatile relationship that was sometimes good and sometimes murderously awful. One of those relationships you don't want to continue, but just can't make yourself leave for inexplicable reasons. Devlin liked the idea of being with someone of obvious wealth and Royal connection, it was as mercenary as that for him. Dom was young and impressionable, he had a privileged life and was finding out who he was and what he wanted out of life. Devlin was somewhat of a rebellious experimental whim for him. He was overwhelmed by the flattery if he analysed it. It was hard to keep up the pretence of having money, but Devlin did his best. The lies he told explaining his wealth at times made him feel guilty. They were a good and honest family as far as he could ascertain and knowing what he had in the bank would not last a lifetime he tried to be frugal whilst putting on a façade of wealth, mainly to impress this new business partner, lover and his wealthy family.

Devlin had 'the look' and the presence to be believed in the circles he was attached to, and he knew it. A tall and handsome man with a tanned skin and chiselled face he attracted attention from both men and women. He often dined alone at one of many of the busy small cafés that nestled into the cool narrow passage-ways of the rambling Old Town, but was never alone for very long, even if that was his preferred choice.

He was content with his own company, sitting in those surroundings with Roman, Moors and Christian architecture all leaving their mark on this part of the Town in spectacular fashion thrilling Devlin each time he looked at it, including the Royal Palace of Almudaina, which is the official residence of the monarchy. He was happy being alone, happy with his own company. Everything else was a bonus.

Palma Old Town, he knew, was steeped in history and Devlin buried himself in those tall, cool stone walls for the best part of ten years. He was hiding in the shadows of former stately homes and some fifty five churches, packed into that tiny part of Palma, buildings dating back to the 17th and 18th century that were scattered in the part of town that Devlin now called home; Stately homes that had been sensitively restored and now used as luxury hotels, their exteriors giving away their ancient history and obvious signs of former economic wealth and Gothic influence, he thought it was a mysterious place and, without a doubt, a great place to disappear.

All of this suited Devlin and he fitted in beautifully. He dressed well and was fun to be around which made him a target for the local party goers, he was always top of the invitation list for social events. He was hiding in plain sight. He never imagined anybody would find him there or link him to the drugs heist in Chale Bay.

Unfortunately, the lifestyle he chose meant he needed money and although he enjoyed spending to keep up the pretence, nice food, socialising, good clothes, it all cost. Mallorca was a very stylish place. Making money on the beach with the tourists was tedious and brought money in, but always at the back of his mind he knew that the huge amount of cash from the Chale Bay Operation was somewhere… but where? Did Maria have it? Matt took a massive amount of money out when he was doing the deals, he must have hidden it away somewhere, surely then, Maria would have access.

She could not have spent it being in prison for the last ten years.

He seemed to have a skill for losing out on money. His partner Martin Squire died leaving him penniless and with nothing from their years of scams and high class robberies they carried out in France, England and the spectacular ones in Russia over a six year period. He tried not to think about the Russian businesses and museums they robbed; Martin was shot getting away from one of them and he nearly died. The others were successful but where were the gems now? Martin died without telling him what he had done with the hoard of diamonds and precious gems they stole during their escapades. He took his eye off the ball and trusted him, Martin assured him their future was safely hidden, then suddenly in a second he was dead, blown to pieces on that boat leaving questions he should have asked but now would never be answered.

Devlin Marshall vowed he would never give up trying to find out, there must be a way, somebody must know something, but as time went on hope faded. This time he would be on top of it and make sure he was the victor.

He had a plan of sorts, and this was the beginning. Devlin wanted more than this hand to mouth existence and the money was running out after ten years. Despite the fact he was with the son of a local aristocrat it bore him no real advantages moneywise. Yes, he was invited to the castle and had access to the motor yacht in the harbour and classy social functions, but he needed money not endless parties and dinners, so he decided the only course of action was to rekindle his friendship with Maria Hayward. She was the key to all of this.

He sent Maria many visiting requests to the prison during the last ten years, all of them declined. But in 1979 suddenly he got an acceptance back from the prison, indicating she would allow him to visit her and so shocked by this Visiting Order he decided to travel back to England, but not through the usual route. He suspected he would still be on a 'wanted' list by Interpol so knew he could not take the risk of a normal flight or any form of customs scrutiny. Not wanting anyone to track him or know where he was he drew up a plan in his head, to sail in some style, back to England to see Maria and get some answers.

There were boats in the harbour, and he could steal one and sail any of them. He made his getaway after the Chale Bay heist in a speed boat, being resourceful he could handle most craft. In the ten years in Palma he had been on board many of these luxury boats and for whatever reason, maybe an unconscious decision, to go back and find the lost money he made it his mission to learn all he could about navigation. The obvious boat was Dominic's family cruiser. He had sailed on it many times and access was easy for Devlin. He could take it and then return it; there would be trouble, but he could face that. If his plan worked he may never return to Mallorca. A problem he would deal with later. Now, the immediate task was to just plan it and do it.

The dilemma he had was whether to include Dominic in his plans. If Dominic was with him the blame could be focussed on him as it was his family who owned the boat. But could he trust him to go with him and keep his mouth shut? That was the 64 thousand dollar question.

Things were not really going well with them, to some extent they were living a lie. Although a relationship had developed quickly between them and for the majority of the time life was great, what they had in the beginning had gone; something was missing and Devlin even doubted that Dom wanted to be with him, or with any man. They socialised with the best on the island, they worked well together in the business but Dominic's father knew nothing of his attraction to men and so they had kept it quiet. Dom flirted with girls at every party and social function, driving Devlin to distraction on occasions. They argued a lot and at times physically fighting in rage.

Ten years down the line they were still together playing this 'are they are they not' game and it was becoming boring. Should he just go back to England alone and do this or drag him along and be constantly looking over his shoulder, wondering if he could trust him, even after ten years he had massive doubts. Lately he had thought of nothing else but his former life that was exciting and at times dangerous. A life where he had some skill and power over others. Training fit men to do dangerous deeds and under thrilling pressure. He was dying here in the sun… withering under the blue skies day after day. Yes it was paradise in the sunshine, but he needed more.

The decision was made one Friday night towards the end of the summer season, during yet another weekend party on the balcony of a beach front apartment. Entertainment was provided by live music from a local trio, dancing, and a hoard of beautiful people draped over each other and drinking as if there would be a shortage anytime soon; Devlin looked around and realised enough was enough. He was done with this lifestyle, of these shallow people who did not live life in the real world but through a haze of booze and drugs. Who were they? He had no idea, faceless self-centred well-kept tanned bodies with very little of interest to talk about. He could not count a single friend amongst them and what was the point of that. He was not getting any younger and maybe wanted somebody by his side who had some substance and a brain. He smiled to himself at that thought. After all this time he realised he just wanted somebody with a brain!

Dominic, true to form, had been openly flirting with a dark haired girl since they got there an hour or so ago, he thought he heard somebody introduce her as Rebecca, Rebecca Nelson? He had seen Dominic with her before at other parties. A beautiful girl who could have chosen any man at any party, but she had her sights on Dominic and he played right into her hands. Devlin watched him operate, who was he trying to fool? Himself? Or maybe he was being honest, and his real preference was to be with women. It had happened too many times for Devlin to believe it was playing to the crowd.

The air was warm and the beach in front of the apartment was almost deserted now with the sun going down in spectacular fashion, with the colours of the sky and sea merging in that stunning magical way that tricks the brain into thinking it is the best sunset ever to emerge on the horizon, when that urge to take a photograph is overwhelming, and then the next one appears, and it happens all over again, like an endless free spectacular.   Drinks were flowing and by 11 most at the party were draped on sofas or lying on the balcony in a slow motion of intoxication or drug induced slumping.   A few stalwarts were still dancing, but slower and with erotic overtones, leaving very little to the imagination. Even the band sounded bored.

Devlin was sober. This was the moment he had wanted to happen. That pivotal moment when the brain gets a mystical message completely out of the blue, for no reason, that just says 'this is that moment' go and do this.

All the cogs and wheels seemed to line up and the mental machinery was in order. The summer was ending, he and Dom were not as strong as they should be, money was running out and he was bored. His heart leapt in his chest as he made the decision; that stomach churning moment that starts or ends events in your life, right or wrong it just happens, and it is like a runaway train...no brakes. He looked around but Dominic was nowhere to be seen, the dark haired girl had also melted into the abyss. Just realising Dom was missing made him feel sick and more than a little angry. He imagined they were in a bedroom in the building or had sloped off somewhere, but Devlin was not going to look.   That was it, the final straw, time to get a grip, and get out of this.

Ten years is enough. He had been thinking about Martin Squire today, the real love of his life, blown to pieces on that boat in Cowes harbour in 1969. He just sat on the beach with tears running down his face, the gut wrenching sorrow came out of nowhere. He had never eradicated that memory or forgotten Martin and wanted either to be alone or find something that came close to the relationship he had with his wonderful clever, eccentric, beautiful Martin. He took a deep breath that was so full of emotion those tears appeared on his cheek, the first he had shed since he died in 1969. Real love has the power to stay inside, tucked away and hidden for sure, but still there… always. He left the apartment, ran down the glass lined staircase and into the warm night air, walking home alone to think.

His heart was racing, At that moment it was difficult to decide which would win, his random, reckless heart or his spinning head.

CHAPTER 3

Harbouring a deep discontent with his life, inwardly hating every day now he was spending with Dominic, knowing they had both lost interest in their relationship and trying to eke out what had become a boring existence working on the beach, he started to be practical by planning for better things for himself. There was no deadline in his head or diary, he knew the right moment would just happen.

He had sorted certain things in his apartment, paying rent up front so he had somewhere to return if it all failed in England, making sure his clothes were ready for a quick departure. His real passport was still just about valid, and he had a fake one with years left on it, just in case he needed to risk going through the proper channels. All he had to do was put on the black clothes similar to those he wore on the Chale Bay heist so he would be harder to see at night, pick up one packed bag, and go.

He decided to wait until 1 am thinking that Dominic might return and for some random reason suddenly agree go with him, even though he had not mentioned one word of this plan to Dom. He had no idea what he would say to Dom if he appeared now. Would he take him or not?…Devlin paced up and down on the balcony of the apartment, listening to the noises creating the night-time atmosphere going past the building. People laughing and enjoying the balmy air, girls giggled, and men shouted with bravado to their friends. That deadline was here, so, at roughly two minutes to one with no sign of

Dom, he scribbled a quick note, in chalk on the board in the kitchen...

'See you in a few days something urgent came up don't worry D'

No kisses no froth, just a basic note, left out of courtesy, after ten years that was the least he could do. He wasn't even sure that Dom would even care he had gone. He left the building, staying in the shadows until he reached the harbour. The streets were almost deserted anyway so he felt sure nobody would see him. There was an eerie stillness and his footsteps the only sound echoing around the narrow passageways that led him down to the Marina, past closed shutters on empty cafés and bars. Even the gnarled ancient olive trees in the square seemed to have a reverent silence about them, not even a rustle of leaves broke the silence.

The motor yacht was a 40 metre beauty, built by Feadship it glowed sleek white with its stylish tinted windows glinting in the moonlight. He knew how to make this baby move as he had taken it for many trips with Dom and his family. There was slight guilt that he was not asking permission to take it, but needs must, and he needed to see Maria. His heart was pounding but he felt alive for the first time in a very long time. His adrenalin was going through the roof; he would need that rush to stay awake for the journey and for that he was relieved, that he felt something at last, even if it was slightly bordering on fear.

He found the key and slowly eased the boat out of the Marina, he had his chart and knew the route, prepared to sail all night and head for Chichester Harbour in England. The prison was just north of

Chichester, he needed to be there in 5 days.

He was glad the yacht was full of diesel, Dom's father was a stickler for keeping it ready for action so with one quick check of the fuel dial he opened her up as soon as he was away from the harbour and out in the open sea. There was a supply of back up fuel onboard so he would maybe only have to stop to refuel once, and he would do that at night. He checked that the last time he was on board and asked Dom's father about how much he kept on board. More than enough to get him well away from Mallorca. It felt good to be away and free.

Half an hour into the trip Devlin thought he heard voices and shouting above the sound of the engine. He checked the radio and that was silent, he slowed down so he could listen… Surely he was imagining it. He put the boat on auto pilot and stepped out onto the deck.

The cabin door opened in front of him, and a male figure staggered out, losing his footing in the gloom he almost landed at Devlin's feet. Very quickly they both realised who they were staring at.

"What the f.*k?!" exclaimed the naked figure of Dominic Montpelier.

"What the f.*k indeed!" retorted Devlin, shocked at seeing his partner, for the last ten years, standing there on the deck on the yacht sailing in the middle of the night in the middle of the ocean stark naked.

"What the hell are you doing? And where are you going?"

demanded Dom, grabbing a towel from a chair and wrapping it around his waist. A voice behind him made them both look back at the door and the dark haired girl from the party emerged, equally naked and rubbing her eyes in an effort to focus in the gloom.

"Dom, where are you? come back to bed, bring me a drink…" she stopped speaking as she noticed the two figures in front of her.

"Dom? Where are you? what's going on? Why are we moving? I need to go home," she was suddenly concerned and even in her drunken state, knew something was not right here.

"Go back down to the cabin Rebecca, I'll be right there, we are going home," he looked straight at Devlin as he spoke in defiance.

"You b*stard Dom, what are you doing…AGAIN! God I am a fool to put up with you. Do you never stop?" We are not going home – I have something to do and now you are coming with me. We are too far out to go back," he was being quite firm and as Dom took in this statement he stumbled as the boat rocked and fell towards Devlin who pushed him away. Dom reacted to the push, that was not meant in any kind of anger, but a natural reaction to stop him falling. Dom, however, did not see it that way and swung at Devlin, missing his chin by a millimetre and muttering something that sounded like,

"You stole my father's boat, bloody cheek."

"Woa…what was that for?" exclaimed Devlin in shock at the intended violence towards him. Dom came back at him for a second time and swung at Devlin, catching him on the side of the face. Devlin clutched his face and grabbed Dom who pulled back with some force and took a third swing at him, this time bringing his arm right behind him before landing another punch.

Because Rebecca was behind him she caught Dom's elbow as he swung his arm back with some power and speed. It hit her right on her nose, they both heard the crack as his elbow hit her face, and she reeled backwards towards the low rail and went straight over the side into the sea. Both men stopped when they heard her hit the water, and instinctively leaned over the rail, shouting out her name in an effort to let her know they were there and trying pull her back in, but she was gone.

Quick as a flash Devlin threw a lifebelt over the side and screamed at Dom, "Keep a look out I'll bring her round and we can go back for her, throw the other lifebelt out to her," he shouted the order to Dom and ran back to the controls swinging the yacht round as fast as he could at the same time flicking the switch to activate the search lights, but Rebecca was gone.

"She can't swim," wailed Dom who was running up and down in a panic, the towel he was clutching flapping behind him, he resembled a demented bird. Devlin could not believe what he was hearing. He shouted again to Dom to unhook the red and white round life raft instructing him to throw it over the side in an effort to try and put as much as they could into the water should Rebecca be near, but he knew it was pointless. The water was cold, she was drunk and naked and couldn't swim. The odds were not good for her. What to do? They could call the coastguard but that was the last thing Devlin needed. Self-preservation kicked in and he increased the speed on the boat, roaring off towards England. Dominic was shouting at Devlin to stop and keep looking but Devlin was not listening, he was on a mission, and this was an inconvenient distraction. He was mad. Mad with himself for not realising they were on board. Mad that he was now saddled with Dom who was going to be a liability and mad that he could do nothing to help that girl.

Dom was in the cabin pleading with Devlin to stop and go back.

"We can't leave her you b*stard. She's a young girl, she can't swim, help her…stop!" he was screaming at Devlin. Shock had kicked in and he was panicking. Devlin shouted at him to calm down.

"Nothing we can do for her, the cold water will be enough, it's too late Dom, we could look all night and not find her. There is no point. Just calm down…sit down. Get dressed. Get rid of her clothes, all of it. Do SOMETHING…"

"Why did you take the boat? Where are you going in the middle of the night anyway?" Dom asked with some anger in his voice. "Wait till my father hears about this," he was not thinking straight and suddenly, to Devlin he sounded like a little boy.

"Nobody will know about this do you hear me? Who knew you were on board with her?"

Dom looked up at him in disbelief at his coldness. "What do you mean who knew we were on board? Well nobody I don't think. I didn't tell anybody we just walked to the boat and got on it."

"Who will miss her? Who is she? Where did you meet? Who knows you were together tonight, did anybody at that gathering actually know your names?"

"Erm, she is…erm, I don't really know. Short name…Becca, Rebecca Nelson I think, I don't know her really," he was struggling to think straight.

"Well THINK and think fast. Who will miss her? Does she live or work locally? Come on Dom THINK," Devlin was demanding some answers. Just to keep the conversation going and make him realise that he needed to grasp the seriousness of what had just happened and deal with it now. Dom said no more. He seemed to glaze over and remained silent.

"Well then, nothing to be done, keep your mouth shut do you hear. A murder charge is something you don't want, your family will be horrified if they find out what just happened here," he was matter of fact and Dom was half listening. Rocking backwards and forwards on the bench in the cabin trying to make some sense of what had just happened.

"Over the next few days I have something to do, and you will do what I say. As far as I can see you and I are done, you have made it clear that you are not interested in me any more so just keep quiet and wait for me to tell you what happens next – do you hear me?" Devlin was being firm and sounded in control. Dom just shook his head in disbelief.

"Murder?" Dom looked stunned. "Murder! It wasn't murder, I didn't know she was behind me. It was an accident."

"Well she is dead, and you did it. I know that and you know that. This is a mess, and I am sorry you are involved in this trip, but you are, so nothing I can do about that right now. When we get to England you will stay on this boat while I do what I need to and then we will see what happens next do you hear me?" His tone had become slightly more threatening, and Dom just stared at the floor, saying nothing. He did not know what to do or think, he was in shock. The girl had not deserved that, and he felt sick. He stood up and went to the edge of the boat and threw up, twice. He crumpled up in a heap and slumped onto a bench on the deck clutching the towel around his shoulders for comfort more than warmth.

Rebecca gone, it happened so quick and now he would have to live with that. But how? He was not sure he could.

"Go and get her stuff and bring it to me," Devlin demanded. "NOW!" He was shouting at Dom who was still in a daze and hadn't moved from the deck in more than an hour.

"I need to sleep," moaned Dom who was still feeling the effects of the alcohol he had consumed earlier. Although it was wearing off he didn't feel right and just clutched the bench and the towel, his knuckles white and his face drained of colour.

"You sleep when we have cleared that girls stuff and thrown it overboard. Bring it here to me. Does she have a bag? I need to look and see if there are any clues as to who she is Dom, GO!"

Dom got up like a robot and walked, across the deck and down the steps into the lower deck. A couple of minutes later he appeared clutching just a dress and a small bag. He unceremoniously dumped it at Devlin's feet. Devlin looked at Dom and at the same time picked up the bag and opened it. His face also drained of all colour, he froze at what he saw and what he read inside the small Chanel bag.

'Sh*t.'

CHAPTER 4

After listening to Maria's account of how Matt had tried to burn her alive in her own house, Devlin quickly changed his attitude during his conversation with her.

"Wow, now I have some understanding of why you acted like you did! What a shock. I would never in a million years imagine him doing that to you. He must have been having some kind of breakdown, maybe the pressure got to him. That is not the Matt I knew, he only had good things to say about you," he stopped, waiting to hear her reply.

It wasn't actually true to say that. Matt indeed was fed up with her, he and Martin Squire had conversations with Matt about her and he definitely wanted out of the relationship but trying to kill her in a burning house was extreme.

Martin met Matt on his own several times, but he never knew why except he didn't think it was to discuss Maria. Devlin had not thought about those Martin-Matt meetings for so many years he had forgotten they happened. Funny how one situation sparks thoughts of another, and he was racking his brains trying to remember why Martin had meetings with Matt. Did he know and had forgotten? Or didn't he know at the time? Martin was not involved with the Organisation at all, and he knew Maria set her sights on him, but he was not interested and told her so. He knew he was walking on egg-shells with her now and needed to keep talking. Get her onside.

"What about the house Maria? Will you have it rebuilt and move back in when you get out, or move away? If I can help I will. I know we didn't leave it on a very good note, but time has passed, and we have all grown up a bit and I'm at a real loose end right now, that's my offer."

He had no idea how she would respond, you just never knew with Maria who had a reputation for blowing hot and cold in the same sentence; but he held his breath and was surprised at her response and revelation about the house.

"The house has been rebuilt."

"How did you manage that?" Devlin was shocked.

"I got my solicitor to arrange it all, it was simple actually, he got an architect and builder, and the insurance money paid for all of it, including his ridiculous fees," she sounded so calm and matter of fact while explaining.

"Well good for you, must be a nice feeling knowing you have somewhere to go back to when you get out of here."

"I am just glad it was all in my name and not his 'cos he paid no attention small details like insurance, live for the day that was his motto," she took a deep breath as if remembering.

"I have been assured it's ready to move back into. Not sure how I feel about that, but I have to go somewhere before I decide what to do when I'm out of here," she sounded sad to talk about the house but continued.

"I can only imagine what it looks like now, I've seen a couple of photos of course but it has all been done without me and I am grateful for a roof over my head when I leave here. It was done years ago and has just been sitting there, empty. The Solicitors firm go and check the post and make sure the house is secure, but nobody has lived there."

He thought he detected a touch of the old Maria, organised, lighter and more positive.

This was like a gift, something he hadn't even thought about on his trip back to England. Funny how things just happen when you least expect them to. He needed somewhere to hide, and even more so now since the tragedy on board the yacht. He had envisaged a pile of rubble smoking in the woods, not a ready built, empty house... This could be the answer to his prayers.

An idea came to Devlin as he sat there listening to her talk about the house. Should he suggest it? What would she say? He had nothing to lose.

"I could go and check it out for you. Maybe stay there and open it up for you, I have nothing planned for the next few months. What do you think?"

Maria looked at him thinking what a cheek! He marches in here and offers to move into my house. MY f**..g house!!! Damn him. But a sudden glimmer of the positive past came into her head. I can handle him, I could cope with him being there. Having somebody like him in the house might afford me some protection. Security...security, that word was always on her mind, back then, certainly now and absolutely in the future she would need somebody. She would be too vulnerable up there on her own. There was always the possibility that the Cartels would come after her for money after the failed heist. There was a huge unpaid debt to that Cartel in New Mexico, and they didn't forget. She looked up at him.

"Ok, I could do that, you could do that. Just come back here regularly and tell me what's happening until I get out, if you don't I'll have you thrown out, I still have connections," she was firm and waited. He hesitated for what he thought was enough time to show her that he had considered it, twisting his face into a pose that would have made the statue of The Thinker jealous.

"Deal, I can do that. I think we need to be friends Maria. Neither of us have that many people in our lives and we do have history together, stuff we need to keep between us. This makes sense on so many levels," he had barely finished speaking when the bell above his head started to ring, indicating the visit had ended. Maria had time to tell him the key to the house was in a box around the back of the house on a shelf above the kitchen door. She had no idea what that meant ' box above the back door'. A door she had never seen but this information had been given to her quite a few times since the house got rebuilt. He left her sitting there almost as stunned as he was but for very different reasons.

He had his 'get out of jail' card; somewhere to hide. Now he could avoid going back to Palma for the time being at least. He still had two major problems, the yacht and Dominic, both needed a lot of thought. The yacht was not a huge problem, he could deal with that, Dom was quite another. What would he do with him? It was paramount that he kept him close for now, using emotional blackmail if necessary to make sure he said nothing.   Dom was terrified enough right now but that shock might wear off and if he tried to get back home or open his mouth they could both find themselves in hot water. Rebecca going overboard was an accident but that was now getting lost as time went on, they didn't report it which would go against them so, they needed to say nothing.

Dom was waiting for him back on the boat in the Marina in Chichester Harbour. He was still in a state of shock after the events of the last few days and had not moved from the same spot that he was in when Devlin left for the prison that morning. It was time to be practical and Devlin swung into action. He was surprised at his reaction to the events this week, Dom was not the strongest person he had ever known but he seemed to be shrivelling in front of his eyes mentally and physically. A thought in Devlin's head was growing by the hour, that if Dom didn't get a grip on this situation they found themselves in, he would be a huge liability to both of them. After the discovery in Rebecca 's bag that shocked Devlin he knew he had to do something drastic. She was Official, his guess was British police or MI5, the identity card and the small pistol he saw in her bag led him to believe that. He wished he had kept both and taken more notice, but in his own panic he threw the bag and I.D card overboard. It was even more crucial that nothing was ever discovered about her demise.

His brain went into overdrive as they left Chichester Harbour to sail across to the Isle of Wight.

They could sail to the Island and put the boat either in a Marina or just risk it and leave it off-shore. Another problem to consider... they just kept on coming. Common sense told him he might need the boat to get away at some point, so abandoning it wasn't on the cards yet. Should he just get rid of Dom in the middle of the Solent? It would be easy...

CHAPTER 5

Maria and Mike Haywards house, burnt to the ground in 1969, but was rebuilt and looked magnificent; it had been standing empty for nearly six years. Maria decided to keep the name. She toyed with a new name, 'Cinders' which appealed to her dark sense of humour but was talked out of it. A new name plate was now in place to the right of the front door in black letters on a once shiny square of brass The Copse.

Jessica was still living in The Old Mill House next door to Maria's house in the woods - with her husband Alex McFarlane and step-daughter Daisy who was now 25 years old. Daisy had trained to be a Solicitor after taking a law degree and had an office in Newport on the Island, she still had a couple of exams to pass but the office had been set up for her by her father. Not quite fully qualified she relied on one other Solicitor Elizabeth Godwin, who had been practising for some years; Daisy was the boss, an odd situation but Elizabeth accepted it.

She spent a lot of time with Jess and Alex, being with them at every opportunity, she loved their company. Alex bought Daisy a waterfront apartment in Cowes as an investment, ten years before, giving it to her for her 21st birthday. Jess was surprised as she had no idea he had purchased the property but accepted it without question. He had a kind heart. Daisy sometimes stayed there, usually at the weekend if she had friends to stay, but mostly it stayed empty.

He owned four apartments in that block, bought with money he took from deposit boxes In Zurich. Money that Matt Hayward had stashed away but never got to use. Jess knew nothing about the other three apartments. He would never be able to explain where he got the money to buy them, glad and relieved she never questioned him, remaining in total ignorance. There were a lot of things that Jess did not know about her wonderful Alex. He led somewhat of a double life, luckily for him she wasn't the inquisitive type, so he kept things simple and said nothing to her.

Jess bought Old Mill House in 1969 and married Alex a few months later. The wedding was months after Maria shot Matt in the kitchen of the Old Mill House. They thought about moving out after the shocking death of Matt Hayward on their kitchen floor, but they both loved the house, and Daisy begged them not to move so they all made the decision to stay.

Jess had wanted to go and visit Maria many times over the last ten years but could not get past the fact she had killed Matt right there, in front of them. She knew it would be a very difficult conversation, so she left everything unsaid and questions unanswered.

Jess had been friends with both of them, staying at The Copse many times before she purchased the Old Mill House. She had an affair with Matt that lasted for the best part of five years, all the time thinking he was married to Maria, but in the end that was a lie. They were only business partners and for some inexplicable reason they both let Jess, and the world, think they were married. Jess was shocked to the core when she found out, but even after that revelation, despite his faults and lies, Matt did not deserve to die like that in cold blood without a chance. To this day she had no idea what made Maria do that to him. It was nothing to do with their affair she was sure of that. Alex thought it was about money, but it was a mystery. Even the court case did not clear things up. Maria said very little during the hearing.

It haunted her if she was honest and often thought about that dreadful night when Maria, just came into her house and shot him. She stood in the living room and aimed her gun through the kitchen door, one shot and he was dead.

It had been hard to get over such a traumatic event, but her life had moved on, their lives were busy and happy. That incident was locked away somewhere in a corner of her brain and knew it would only come out again if she ever saw Maria again.

Jess and Alex had no children, it just never happened, so Daisy was their world, and they made a formidable trio. There were rumours about The Copse, and because of Alex's job, now more MI5 than MI6, she was able to be kept informed about what was happening to Maria in prison and her appeals. Jess knew that one day she would face Maria, one day she would probably be walking in the village or up through the woods or on one of her runs and inevitably they would meet again, it was a small place.

Alex had told her a lot about his job and the search for the people who smuggled in drugs and arms to the Island. They suspected Maria was one of the OCG (organised crime gang), a major player, but they couldn't prove it.   He said it was only a matter of time before they got enough evidence, and they would never let it go.

Walking through the village and up through the woods as she usually did several times a week, she was curious to see lights on in The Copse and wandered close enough to see through the window.

She had seen people there many times over the years, watching the rubble from the old house being removed and the horror when the demolition crew found the skeletons of two bodies in the rubble bringing up more unanswered questions, then the new house being built. She had asked enough questions during the reconstruction of the house and found out it was a legal firm that acted for Maria who kept any eye on the place, but she had never seen anybody here this late in the day.

The house was now very different to the old rambling house that hid a gruesome secret wing before the fire. It now had the look of a huge glass box, very modern design with massive picture windows. The new house demanded attention and almost boasted the shiny glass balcony at the front that overlooked the garden with views right down to the cliffs and the sea. The glass reflected the countryside and the magnificent trees, blending it into the landscape in a breath-taking way. It wasn't her style at all, preferring the Old Mill House with its thick walls, traditional windows and history, but Jess had to admit it was beautiful in its own way.

She recognised the man inside the house, and it wasn't the usual old boy who came to pick up post and check the locks...' Oh my God is that Devlin Marshall?'

How could she forget him? Even after such a short introduction and the dinner party at The Copse, back in 1969; that dreadful dinner party when he came to visit with Martin somebody, she couldn't remember his name but remembered he wore lots of jewellery… She ran back to the Old Mill House to tell Alex what she had just seen.

When she got back to the Old Mill House she was out of breath and annoyed with herself that she had not just tapped on the window and said hello. Why wouldn't she do that? It was no secret she knew Maria and she had met Devlin in the old house.

"Alex, Alex…" No response, where was he? She ran out of the kitchen door and up into the garden that was on a higher level than the house and found him in one of the outbuildings, doing something technical to the engine of the lawn mower.

"Guess who I just saw up at The Copse?"

"I give up," he laughed without even guessing.

"Devlin Marshall! Remember me talking about him all those years ago? Heaven knows why I remember him, but I do, and he is inside The Copse right now!"

"Are you sure? What were you doing up there?" He was interested for sure and he wiped his oily hands on a cloth and looked at Jess, waiting for an answer. Jess laughed as he spoke, not sure why he was asking her that question. She often wandered up into the woods and he knew that.

"No reason, you know I often go up there, and yes I am sure it was him, he is very distinctive and hasn't changed much since last I saw him. It's all glass up there now and easy to see in. Don't think he saw me though, I was behind a tree," she laughed. "I felt like a spy, lurking behind that huge oak up there!"

"Well I wonder why he has turned up? Maybe because Maria has her Parole appeal coming up, wonder if they have kept in touch, well stupid statement, of course they must have, or he wouldn't be in there would he?" he answered his own question.

"Well I will go back tomorrow and knock on the door, not sure why I didn't just now, I did know him back then and I could have asked him about Maria, he might tell me why he is there. What do you think? Wouldn't hurt would it to go and find out?" She had made up her mind and it didn't matter what Alex said to her, nothing would stop her going back up there with or without his approval.

Knowing what he needed to do, and a feeling of what he would actually do about Devlin Marshall, because he was still on the wanted list by Interpol even ten years later. Alex was not going to encourage Jess to speak to him, but he was curious; having him back in England might be complicated. He never thought he would dare show his face here again. Alex knew he could keep an eye on the visit, so his response was cautiously positive.

"Well if you are careful. Not sure what he is like these days. We had people keeping an eye on him in Spain, that's where he has been all these years. We finally found him about a year ago. He went off the radar after Chale Bay in 69, and we still want to talk to him, but I guess if I keep an eye it might be interesting," Alex finished speaking and decided he would go himself and have a look when it was dark, just to quell his curiosity and confirm it was Devlin

Marshall if nothing else. It had been a long time since their paths had crossed. Marshall used to operate with Martin Squire, mainly jewellery theft on a grand scale. Squire was killed on the boat in Cowes Harbour on fireworks night in 1969, he had told Jess the story many times but refreshed himself by going over it again in his head. Why is he back? That was the burning question.

"Will you have to report this?" Jess asked fearing the old problems would be rearing up again in this sleepy place.

"Probably, but I will go and have a look first," Alex replied, knowing he would have to be very careful with this information. He would sit on it for a while. The last thing he wanted was a swarm of police coming here and raiding next door. For now he would keep it to himself. Things were more complicated now some of his estranged family had been in touch again and he was looking for the right moment to mention certain things he had going on to Jess, he was walking in two worlds right now but he needed to keep an eye on what was happening so he could not be accused of failing in his duty…

True to his word, when it was dark and Jess was in bed, Alex slipped out of the Old Mill House with his long lens camera and binoculars, he made his way up to The Copse.

He stopped by the huge Oak tree that Jess had mentioned earlier, out of sight of the house but a good vantage point to aim his long lens. There appeared to be just two people in the house, Devlin Marshall and a younger, dark haired man that Alex did not recognise. Nothing much to see, they did not get close to each other, mostly sitting in the living room or one or other of them going into the kitchen. He stayed there for half an hour and got his pictures, making a mental note to come back and take more, maybe during the day when they might have visitors.

Next day Jess was up and ready to go after breakfast, but she waited until mid- morning before going up to The Copse, just in case Devlin was not an early riser. She was assuming he was staying at the house and would be there this morning, indeed she wasn't disappointed as she walked up the driveway and saw him standing on the glass balcony looking out and straight at her. He moved away from the window which, for a few minutes made Jess wonder if he was trying to avoid visitors, or maybe just her, but the massive shiny black front door opened; he stood there with a huge grin on his face. Definitely a grin of recognition welcoming her like an old friend. Two kisses on either side of her face which was very European to Jess.

"Well well, this is a blast from the past," he exclaimed, and seemed pleased to see her. If not he is a very good actor she thought.

"Long time no see," was the only thing Jess could think of at that moment. What do you say to somebody you don't really know in such circumstances. She would have to think on her feet and quick to get the best out of this meeting.

"Jess isn't it?" he remembered her name, she hadn't changed at all, even in ten years she was still stunning with that long red hair, gleaming in the sunlight.

"Yes, well remembered! I was walking past the other day, and

I thought I recognised you. I should have called in then but had an appointment I couldn't miss," she lied.

He invited Jess inside; she was soon exclaiming how she couldn't believe how beautiful the interior was, and how different from the old rambling house that had stood on that very spot some ten years before. It was flooded with light, with huge windows bringing the trees and countryside inside the house in an illusion of space. There were no curtains or blinds at the windows, nowhere to hide in here was her first thought. Jess asked after Maria, thinking it would be odd if she didn't, but Devlin said very little, only that he had seen her, and she was well and hoping to be out soon after a Parole appeal. He made no mention of why he was there.

He gave her a tour of the house and they stopped to talk on the glass balcony at the front of the house, it was attached to the huge master bedroom. There was a king sized bed in the room and a desk with a tall black leather chair facing the huge window. There were three telephones on the desk which Jess thought was odd. She double checked cables running to the floor to confirm they were working phones. It looked as if he was staying there as there were some clues to his presence. There were no cupboards or drawers in the room and clothes lay on the floor, but neatly folded; a few bottles were lined up neatly in the en-suite bathroom but very little else. One of the bedroom doors was closed and she wasn't shown that room. She thought she counted five or six bedrooms. It became obvious why when they went back downstairs, and a man appeared.

"Jess this is a friend of mine, Dominic Montpelier," he said it very quickly, just a simple introduction, she hardly caught his second name. Jess shook his hand which was limp and indifferent, was that French? His surname sounded French. There was no eye contact and Jess felt he was less than pleased to see her there. There was an apologetic air about him. Difficult to put into words. He was very good looking, with an air of Spanish about him, dark and European, a little like her Alex when he was younger.

They chatted about Maria, and it was clear that Devlin would stay there for the foreseeable future, at least until Maria was released which could be very soon if her Parole appeal was successful. He gave little away, just saying he was doing her a favour by keeping an eye on the place and getting some more bits of furniture and stocking up the kitchen for her. He said nothing about the last ten years, and she didn't ask. He didn't explain who Dom was, and there was no conversation back from him, not a word followed the forced 'hello.' He made them all tea and put it on the table and left her with Devlin. Jess thought he seemed dead behind his eyes somehow. She tried to explain to Alex when she returned to the Old Mill House.

"You have done WHAT?!!!" exclaimed Alex when she returned.

"I have invited them both over on Saturday for drinks. I thought we could get to know them as they are staying for a while. Doesn't have to be formal, can just get some nibbles and a few bottles of wine," she seemed pleased with herself. He wasn't so sure.

"What is he like?" Alex was curious.

"Devlin? mmmm Devlin Marshall, well, I never really liked him if I am honest. If I remember correctly he wasn't very pleasant to me when he came to that dinner party with Martin whatshisname," Alex chipped in, "Squire... Martin Squire, no idea why I remember his name, but I do."

Jess continued, "I did take an instant dislike to him, however, he wasn't so awful today seemed more mellow somehow. Guarded I would say... not giving too much away. He seemed pleased to see me, but I can't think why. The younger one, Dominic, what was his second name, French sounding Montpelier I think he said, he was strange. Didn't seem to be there somehow, glazed over and definitely not pleased to see me, maybe on drugs. Will be interesting if nothing else!" Jess was curious now and wanted to know more. He bothered her, the younger one, although not that young twenty eight maybe, thirty maximum. Somehow it felt as if he was there under duress and didn't want to be... but surely that couldn't be right. Her instincts were usually right, she had a natural intuitive nature, so she looked forward to a bit more digging at the weekend.

Devlin had bigger plans than an invitation to drinks next door. He wasn't sure why he agreed to go, clearly curiosity was in the air for all of them. His brain was going a hundred miles per hour, fired up with plans since he saw Maria in the prison and got her permission to move into The Copse.

His focus was on contacting his former colleagues in Paris and London now he had a base, knowing he could rebuild a team that he trusted and set up more deals.   Who would suspect another drugs drop on the Island? Would he dare use Chale Beach again? He had the contacts, only a few were arrested the last time and they said nothing; most escaped. He had the guts to do it. Boredom ate into your head, and he was no good earning pennies from the beach. All that was a waste of time and where had it got him? A useless partner upstairs that had turned into a liability. He would deal with Dom, he was not sure how yet, but he would have to. He had the pistol from that girls bag. It crossed his mind more than once.

Maria would be back, and he felt she would be more than up for continuing where she left off, he just hoped she would be with him and his plans.   He arranged meetings for the next couple of weeks and the frustration would be having to wait for it to start to happen. Surprisingly, things moved faster than expected, people were being positive about another go at Chale Bay, and before long the phones were ringing all the time, the office set up in the master bedroom became the focus of activity in the house. It was the best view in the house, and he enjoyed sitting at that desk looking out towards Culver Cliff and planning his future.

This felt like the right place and the right time, he was invigorated by this house, its seclusion and dominant location. It gave him a feeling of power looking down on the world from up there on his glass 'cloud.' Dom became domesticated and silent, he felt as if he was invisible which suited him.   Devlin ignored him mostly, but at the same time he was watching his every move, so he just pottered around cooking and wiping surfaces. He seemed unable to get a grip on this new reality. If there was such a thing as polar opposites, then they were it.

Devlin told Dom nothing of what he was planning. He knew nothing of the events of 1969 or any previous deals involving Chale Bay, and that was how it was going to stay. Devlin just didn't trust him, he meant no harm, but he had no filter and never thought of the consequences of saying too much, on reflection he never did; he was glad he had kept the whole Chale Bay Operation from ten years ago a secret from him, a man he thought was strong and reliable in the beginning had melted into a shadow in a few days and as the days slipped away he was making it clear he was surely a burden to him and his plans.

Word spread fast that the old team were re-forming, with Devlin and Maria once more at the helm. Times were hard and people wanted a chance to make some money. They did it before, some got caught, but most escaped. Gossip went through Paris and London like a rocket and people he thought would never consider being available for another drugs heist, started to crawl out of the woodwork and make themselves available. The speed of it took him by surprise, so to give himself an evening off and a few hours to chill and think, he and Dom drove down to Chale to Devlin's favourite pub, The White Mouse Inn.

After a wonderful meal of the finest seafood, they even talked to each other and laughed. It was like the old days. Devlin even questioned his own judgement, could he trust Dom? Should he trust him? Maybe he was wrong, and he would come out of the shock soon. He would have to make some decisions. It would be easy to dispose of him in a country lane on South Wight, it was so isolated in parts. The thought crossed Devlin's mind as they drove back in the dark. He patted his inside pocket to reassure himself he still had the gun. But the tension they were feeling after the boat and the girl seemed to have melted into a bit of peace and tranquillity in the pub, so Devlin put that idea away for now, and they enjoyed a slow drive back to The Copse.

A distant thunderstorm lit up the horizon as they drove back over Luccombe towards Shanklin, and Culver Cliff appeared out of the black sky exposed by the sudden flashes of lightning, reminding Devlin what a wonderful and dramatic place this island could be at times, especially during thunderstorms.

Their peaceful evening was brought to an abrupt halt, however when Devlin opened the front door. The alarm failed to go off, and he knew immediately that wasn't right. He set the alarm himself before they left, so why was it silent? He reached to his inside pocket for his gun and grabbed Dom's arm, indicating that he should stand still while he went to investigate. All the lights were off, so he flicked the switch in the hall that flooded the living room with light. He was shocked to see, sitting in the dark, unannounced and not invited, two male visitors.

How did they get through the door without the alarm system alerting the whole village? Devlin would have to sort that one out but suspected his visitor's previous life of crime provided the knowledge to override a simple thing like a burglar alarm. He made a mental note to improve the system.

The scar on his throat was evil, Devlin couldn't take his eyes off it. How could anybody survive that? A question he put to his midnight visitor as he put the gun back in his pocket.

"What the hell are you doing here? I thought you were dead, and you turn up here? How did you get in? Jamal Lesçon… Jamal F**.ng Lesçon! Now there is a face I never thought I would see again, how the hell did you know I was here?" So many questions but Devlin just kept on asking him before he had a chance to say a word. The man with the scar stood up and they hugged each other with the biggest of bear hugs, both overwhelmed to see the other. Then lots of slapping backs and arms, they continued the questions. He had another man with him, a younger man, his son Theo who was tall and athletic. Devlin immediately understood why he used him as his 'wingman', he looked fit and ready to fight. On a first meeting he gave the impression that he would be no pushover in an argument, with serious battle scars on his face and a lot of visible tattoos making him look like someone you would not want to get into a fight with, he had a tough exterior for sure. Jamal Lesçon, the top man in the Paris office before he was unceremoniously and supposedly assassinated by André Sandler's crew. But that attempt clearly failed, he was very much alive and seemingly with a very big axe to grind. He wanted revenge on those people, and he wanted to come back and make money. Life had been hard for him this last ten years recovering from the dreadful night he was attacked and luckily saved by a passing ambulance with a doctor on board. The odds on that were miniscule and he knew it. He lived life to the full and was determined to get back what he lost. He had done his homework and knew about Maria and the house. He had heard Devlin was rounding up the old crew so finding him here was a bonus, he always had great respect for Devlin, he knew he was a man more than capable of handling Maria Hayward.

Maria and Matt had given Jamal the job of running the Paris office all those years ago. He knew Maria would welcome him back. He had contacts and people working for him; people who would come here and continue the work that was smashed by Interpol and the British police back in 1969. Paris could be dangerous place unless you knew the right people and Jamal knew the right people. It was a Cosmopolitan maze of races and cultures all vying for position and hungry for money. Poverty in the City drove men to do unimaginable things but harnessed and guided they could be a force to be reckoned with. He had good contacts with a lot of those people, and he had gained a lot of respect over the years, earned with trust, knowledge and ultimately fear. He knew this time it would be bigger and with his input they could succeed with another Operation to bring them all the money and power he had craved. He kept his fingers in many International pies and now he was here ready to go.

And for his trump card he had brought a formidable Russian with him…

CHAPTER 6

The Paris office where Maria and Matt controlled a legitimate Procurement Company to cover for their illegal dealings in drugs and weapons, was never going to be physically resurrected but the same spirit could rise again like an energised phoenix. All the staff had dispersed to their corners of Paris and beyond but were making very positive noises about loyalty and the desire to regroup as a team. Backed by Jamal Lesçon and Theo they were ready.

André Sandler was dead and good riddance as far as Devlin and Jamal were concerned. He ordered the assassination on Jamal and took over the Paris Office, thinking he could do a better job. Maria ended that dream with Devlin's help, and Sandler was obliterated before he could take over the whole Organisation. Poisoned in his own favourite café, the effects simulated a heart attack resulting in no investigation of his death. He upset too many people including Maria who could be ruthless in a very quiet and deadly way.

She was dangerous and people were very wary of her. She took no prisoners, and you just never knew what she was thinking or going to do next. An unpredictable and practised liar, who only wanted to be kingpin, there was nobody she would not remove if they got in her way. Matt Hayward, her partner for years, paid the ultimate price for his greed and taking his eye of the ball.

Martin Squire paid with his life because he rejected Maria's amorous advances. Innocent people died because she ordered Matts demise, but it went wrong and instead of her hitmen killing Matt, they put explosives on a boat in Cowes Harbour believing Matt was on board and several people totally unconnected with the Organisation, perished in a shocking explosion on fireworks night in August 1969. Devlin Marshall would have been on that boat, but for fate missing a connection in his journey, he was aware of all of this; making him very cautious and determined to stay one step ahead of her. Matt deliberately avoided the boat that night, hearing through his trusted grapevine there was a plot to kill him. There was nothing Devlin wouldn't do to keep her on side. There was already a queue of people who wanted her dead.

The Copse could, no would, be the HQ for everything. Devlin made up his mind about that. Nobody would suspect they would have the nerve to organise another Operation, from the island, let alone this house. It was run from here, in part, back in the 60's with the Paris office a cover for the procurement and importation of legitimate goods and a very small office in Cowes to put up a false front for their illegal business dealings. He could replicate that here and didn't see the point of other premises.

Jamal Lesçon was actually here, in front of him, maybe he could be part of that. But could he trust him? That was the question. He needed somebody to trust and if he had the choice of anybody from the old crew, then Jamal would be the man. He certainly had good reason to get back on top, he certainly had the knowledge and contacts required to help organise such a plan, he could fill in the gaps in Devlin's already encyclopaedic brain. Devlin had no interest in the negotiation part of this, speaking to Cartels and doing deals was not what he wanted to do, so could Jamal be the man for that? Despite everything, Matt did that job for years and was the best. In his bumbling chaotic way he got the best deals out of men who would happily kill you if you looked at them the wrong way. He led a dangerous life but made it look so damned easy.

Maria had selected Jamal to run the Paris office and Devlin had no reason to doubt her instincts so maybe he would agree to stepping into Matt's shoes, if not they had to think fast and find another strong and reliable member of the team. Jamal had contacts and so did Devlin but right now he was struggling to think of anybody who would have the strength of character and be ruthless and fearless enough to be the key negotiator for them. In short they needed someone with balls of steel and who was not afraid of dying! If all else failed he would have to step in. But that was the very last option.

It was starting to take shape. He would go back to see Maria and talk to her about Jamal. Her appeal was coming up in the next couple of weeks so it may be that she would be back before the visiting order could be arranged. He made a mental note to sort the visit tomorrow.

There were six bedrooms in The Copse so plenty of room to use this as the hub of a new plan. Devlin invited Jamal and Theo, to stay for a while and they agreed.

They were talking about Matt and how he had managed the negotiations. Devlin was sounding him out for maybe stepping into the role left by Matt and out of the blue Jamal announced that had brought an acquaintance with him, but he had booked him into a local hotel. He wanted to test the water before bringing him to the house. The plan was to meet him in the next couple of days and find out if Devlin thought he could fit in.

"Look Devlin, I didn't bring him here tonight because I wanted to see what you were planning first, he is a brute of a human being, not like Matt at all but I really think he is the man we need."

"So you are not putting yourself in that role then? Why not? You have the experience and the guts…look what you have been through this last ten years," and he nodded towards his throat.

"No that's not for me, I couldn't do the travelling Matt did because of this, he pointed to the scar on his throat, my health isn't what it was. Matt was a people person, he showed me what was needed to negotiate with these monsters in the Cartels and to be honest with you, we do need more knowledge of the drugs market than I could bring to this and also there is a worldwide need to increase the weapons side of things. There is a huge market right now for Northern Island alone, for small arms, rifles, explosives. We need to fill the gap in the market. So much has gone on there over the last few years, there is a huge demand for guns and explosive devices or the materials to make their bombs, much bigger demand than drugs," he was very compelling with his knowledge, took a breath and continued with his explanation for not wanting to be the negotiator.

"I don't have the contacts for weapons, I have no experience with that side of things, but I know people who do, my friend especially, and as much as the spirit is willing the flesh just hasn't got the strength anymore. I am your logistics man. If it needs organising, I can find men to get it done, if it needs transporting, I can arrange that. I will get things done in the background to make it run as smooth as clockwork," he stopped and took a drink from his cup, leaning back into the chair as if exhausted by the thought of what happened to him ten years ago. That dreadful day in the street, in broad daylight when somebody attacked him from behind with a knife, and he hung on to life by the thinnest of threads for days. He was lucky to be alive and he knew it.

"Nikolai is fearless and people like him and fear him in equal measure, which is important. His bark is worse than his bite, but if push comes to shove he is not afraid to fight for what he wants, he is ruthless, believe me."

"Nikolai? He sounds Russian? Devlin was curious.

"Correct, Moscow, we can arrange to meet him in the next couple of days when you are free?" Jamal was telling Devlin but made it look like a request.

Jamal was very convincing, but Devlin wanted to meet this Russian before making any decisions.

"How do you know him?" a reasonable enough question.

"He came to me recommended by a friend in England, he was in trouble in Russia and needed somewhere for him and his family to hide for a while, he owes me big time," he smiled a contented smile, happy to have saved a man and his family from the jaws of the KGB. What he didn't tell Devlin was that his friend in England was Alex, Alex McFarlane. He didn't need to know that yet or the connection.

Excitement was a strong word to use but Devlin was buzzing with something, maybe anticipation at the prospect of what could emerge from all of this. He wanted this next drugs haul to be the biggest and the last, maybe Jamal was right and there was a huge market to bring in more weapons as well as drugs this time. He was correct in his thinking, the thirst for weapons in Northern Ireland had definitely grown, that thirst had never gone away in ten years. They would have to come and collect them though from the drop off in South Wight when it happened – he would never agree to deliver them to Ireland. Far too dangerous. So much going on in his head and he needed to think and think fast, this was moving at a pace, and he felt overwhelmed by it all, he knew he needed a good team and fast. But now Jamal has said he can handle a huge part of that. Devlin never expected to be ensconced in a house like this and in his wildest imaginings never thought about Jamal Lesçon turning up. He was dead as far as Devlin knew but this was fantastic news. A world of possibilities was opening up in front of him.

It seemed to be clicking into place. He could not do this alone, with Maria on his side maybe she could spring back into action and bring her expertise back, but he didn't trust her just yet. She was such a loose cannon, and he didn't know how her mind was working back then and now with ten years in prison, who knew what she was thinking and how she would deal with these new plans. She would surely be the loosest cannon in the row of cannons he was setting up…

CHAPTER 7

"No, no, a thousand times NO," was the first reaction from Maria when Devlin returned to Blaydorn prison. She was almost struck dumb when Devlin, in a very quiet voice suggested they picked up where they left off in 1969. Ten years is a long time, but he felt it was perfect timing. The authorities would have put all ideas of a similar Operation out of their heads and on such a scale would never occur to them. They could do this because they had the had the expertise between them and clearly getting the manpower together was not proving to be a problem at all.

. It was difficult to talk to her without being heard by the guard that was 15 feet or so away from her, but he leant in close to the glass and so did she. He thought he saw a glimmer of interest from her after her initial negative response, so he kept going with the persuasion. When he told her about the returning Jamal she was understandably stunned.

"He is ALIVE?" she slumped back in her chair. "That is just

not possible."

"As sure as God made little apples, seen him with my own eyes, he is here in England! In your house as a matter of fact, with his son Theo," Devlin was smiling.

"I almost don't believe it – are you sure it's him? I didn't know he had a son," her face was screwed up in disbelief. "How do you know it's him?"

"Remember I knew him, I only met him once, but it's him. He has the scar to prove what happened. It's him alright, as amazing as that is, he has tracked you for years, just waiting to come back. He has a lot of contacts in Paris and Russia that we will need, we have a solid connection with him. You gave him the job in Paris, so he has a lot of respect for you. You trusted him once and I think we should trust him now. Apparently word was out all over Paris I was looking for people again and he knew where you lived. He got a tip off you might be out by now and just went to the house to find out. He broke in cheeky b*stard! He has looked for me for years but couldn't find me, and of course he knew about Matt and Martin Squire. He has more contacts than ever, we have talked briefly and think we could all operate from The Copse. What do you think? Take your time, don't have to decide today, just think about it. But I will say Maria I am doing this with or without you. If you want out we will find another place to use as our HQ," he waited.

In a second she responded. It was as if Devlin had smacked her in the face, she sat up on the short chair and a super speed switch went on in her head. Do it without me? Not a chance... She was mortified he would have the nerve to even think about doing it without her and she challenged the suggestion as soon as he said he would cut her out.

"Don't even think about setting up without me! You and I will lead it, joint partners like I offered before. Either that or nothing." She threw the ultimatum straight back at him, as if he had no choice. The irony of her situation wasn't lost on either of them. As if she could dictate from her position in here, but he was aware of her past and aware of the risk he took if he went against her. "The deal will be that we use The Copse and build a team. You deal with things until I get out of here, 50/50 on decisions," she was firing on all cylinders now.

"We can't do this with just the two of us, not on the scale I am planning," he reminded her.

"Anybody else who comes in will have to earn their place and the pay-outs will be the same as before, well maybe a little more as it has been ten years… percentagewise it will be the same," her voice was low in volume but huge in implication, she had threat in her manner, and he was listening. He heard her, loud and clear, got up and said his goodbyes, knowing he had work to do. He knew there would be another fight for position in such a set up, but he was prepared for it, he had learned a lot in ten years. He knew it would be bigger than a two person operation and she had to adjust her thinking. She was a control freak but that wouldn't work this time, they had to act as a team, if she thought it would be a small as last time and she would be in total control, then she was very mistaken.

Like it or lump it he would be in ultimate command of this with her as an important cog in the wheels, but he needed somebody with the knowledge and circle of contacts like Jamal, and some strength, hopefully if this Russian's reputation was to be believed it might be him joining them. They were yet to meet, and he felt he would know straight away. Jamal's son was an interesting character and liked him more every time they had a conversation, he was intelligent and calm with an air of confidence about him, he looked as if he could handle himself. It would work. He felt it with a rush through his body. That feeling when sex has been absent for a while. He needed this. He had this overwhelming feeling he needed Theo, but this was not the time for that. Just out of one relationship he needed to think about going into another, the pull was strong, but he must resist. For now.

The next few days were manic, he set up a bigger office in the 'balcony room' with a couple of desks and put beds into the five bedrooms with some spare fold up beds for the crew when they gathered just before the next cargo drop. Bedroom 6 was his, it was big enough for two double beds and an office space, the planners had done well, especially with the glass balcony, It felt like a new start, and he would be at the heart of this no matter what he had to do to make it work.

Part of him wanted Maria to be released and part of his brain told him he could do this without her and use Jamal's help. The contacts he had around him and the crew he was gathering, were of the same breed as the ones that worked so well together before. A few were the same men that he had trained for the Chale Bay heist, others came with recommendation. He had provided all those men in 1969 and for years before that for other jobs, so he trusted him to get it right. He may not even have to oversee the training as Jamal's son was quite prepared to take that on. Theo apparently had a military background in France, and he knew he could work with him, he more than liked him. It all started to fall into place at some speed.

Jamal again declined the offer to be the front man for negotiations even with a relayed message request from Maria. He insisted that Devlin considered the Russian, Nikolai Markarov, but he said to call him Nik so nobody realised he was Russian, until he opened his mouth of course, apparently had skin so thick he would make an elephant blush.

He had experience with the KGB and his English was perfect having been educated in an English University. He was on the run himself, there was so much going on in Russia right now, Afghanistan was looming as a world threat and even speaking about it meant he had upset some high up Generals in Moscow. So with threats on his life and to his wife and children, he made the decision and got out, wanting to make a life for himself and his family in a safer country. He got to Europe and made contact with Jamal.

With his help he decided to leave his family in Paris for the time being and join these people in England. In Moscow he was being threatened by phone calls and men following him. The threat was real, and he was taking no chances.

Jamal helped him find refuge in Paris and for that alone, the

Russian was immensely grateful, he said he would work until he dropped, because he was so thankful to have a safe place for his family and to have escaped with his life. He had the contacts, and the language skills; Jamal was going to great lengths convincing Devlin he might be the right man. They were to meet in the next few days, and he would decide. Jamal did not cease to sing his praises at every opportunity. He had better live up to this high praise.

CHAPTER 8

Devlin knew it was dangerous to bring in the Russian, an unknown quantity, but men with the skills they needed were hard to find. He was being hailed as having a reputation for being tough and finding somebody to take Matt's place made Devlin realise how clever he had been all those years bringing in so much business, making it look effortless which it clearly was not. He wished he had known him better but c'est la vie, hindsight is a wonderful thing, sadly too late and nothing could be done about that now. Would this Russian be the one man they were looking for to fill Matt's shoes, could they be that lucky? It was time for taking risks and Devlin was not afraid to do just that.

Matt dealt with dangerous men in Cartels in South America that would kill you soon as look at you. But there never seemed to be any trouble with Matt ostensibly having them in the palm of his hand with not an ounce of trouble. If there was he must have dealt with it. Nothing really ever filtered back to him about issues with the negotiating and dealing, his loss was massive to this Organisation then and would be in the future. Only time would tell if they could replicate everything Matt had done. Each person being key to the smooth running as before.

Devlin had been the one to betray them all because of his own personal grief.

None of the others knew what he had done or why. Maria had no idea he was in a relationship with Martin Squire. Nobody did. They had an exciting and dangerous lifestyle before they got involved with Maria and Matt. They went across Europe ripping off and robbing some of the biggest Stately Homes and museums in Paris and Russia. The diamonds and jewels they stole were worth a fortune. Most of it had been broken down by a contact in Hatton Garden so the gems were mostly taken out of their settings, the rings and necklaces no longer existed leaving just the gems and gold, mostly diamonds. Devlin kept a couple of rings and so did Martin, Art Deco ones they both loved. The loss of Martin made him behave in a way that was destructive and selfish, he knew that now. The loss of all those gems they stole was nothing compared to the loss of Martin. One day he might find out what happened to it all. He trusted Martin with them, and he died not telling Devlin what he had done with them. Where they in a bank somewhere? Did he trust somebody to look after them? He didn't sell them because his bank accounts didn't reflect any wealth. Somebody must know.

But for now, he would rebuild this, bigger and better than before. He had a determination born out of loss and anger and a need for the good life that money would surely bring him. You just don't know what you have got until you lose it, and he still felt that pain even ten years on. A new philosophy for him but he fought to push the past out of his head.

The weekend came and Devlin remembered the invitation to the Old Mill House. An event he could have done without but feeling that he may glean some information about the current state of investigations around the missing money from the Chale Bay heist he arrived with Dom and Jamal and Theo in tow.

Jess was surprised when they walked into the garden, all four men looking less than enthusiastic about the evening ahead in the garden with relative strangers.

Daisy joined them along with her two friends from Uni, Megan Warner and Ruth Springfield, who trailed behind Daisy like puppies. They were good company, Megan was shy but witty and Ruth the life and soul of any party, suddenly it was bigger than Jess had imagined, and with nine people it was more than had ever visited them in ten years at the same time. It made conversation easier with more people and less awkward with not so much focus on Devlin Marshall.

It was warm so thankfully they were able to sit in the garden, it seemed less formal in that setting. Jess had made some food, not too much, but now worried there would not be enough. She was clever enough to make it look casual. There was plenty of beer and wine and the three men added to the collection of bottles arriving with more wine. They discussed various labels on the wine and preferences before they sat around for introductions.

Alex felt all his Christmas's had come in early. Obviously, he knew the name Jamal Lesçon and was interested to see him again. He knew what happened to him after his involvement with the Paris office and he knew Devlin Marshall was connected to all of it but had no idea how Dominic fitted into the group. He hoped that Jamal wouldn't mention knowing him from the Paris office. Alex went in there all those years ago to help with the investigation of the office in Paris when Jamal was in charge. MI6 were convinced it was the cover for some illegal trading but could not find enough evidence in the end. He also knew that Jamal had disappeared and what happened to him, and the office taken over by another man whose name he could not remember.

He was keen to find out who Dominic was. A phone call earlier in the day told him that Dominic Montpelier had no previous record with either the British police or Interpol, but that did not quell his curiosity. There was nothing on Jamal's son either. Unless they operated under the radar.

Daisy was transfixed on Dominic, he was a good looking man but didn't seem to want to be there and it intrigued her. Was he with Devlin? He was hanging on his every word, but not really joining in any of the chatter, Devlin seemed to be watching him but there was no conversation between them which was strange. There were no signs of any kind of relationship, Daisy suspected that Devlin was gay but kept that thought to herself, Jamal was speaking about family, and he didn't chat at all to Dom, they seemed like strangers, so she discounted him as the reason Dom was there. They were a strange bunch which was intriguing for Daisy and certainly for Jess and Alex.

The eye contact between Dominic and Daisy was instantaneous and continued for the whole of the evening. He made the first move towards Daisy as her father watched them like a Hawk, as he walked towards her she stepped forward to speak to him.

"Hi, I'm Daisy," she held out her hand to shake his as he approached her, and he looked surprised at the formality. He hesitated and then grabbed her hand as if it was a lifeline, shaking it feverously.

"Dominic Montpelier, hello," he kept it short.

"French?" enquired Daisy. Dom laughed and replied in the negative, explaining his father was French but he was actually Spanish by birth, but left it at that. He didn't think mentioning Palma or Mallorca was a good idea at this point. He actually failed to see the point of anything right now, with what had happened on the yacht and being dragged here, into the middle of nowhere he felt he had guilty written all over him and he was being held like a prisoner. The shock was wearing off and he was starting to think for himself at last. He was very glad to be here with new company and an attractive woman to talk to. Three attractive women, but it was Daisy who caught his attention. She was stunningly beautiful, a really natural looking girl, tall and slim with dark brown hair that swung in the light breeze and a smile that lit up the conversation and his, current, miserable world.

"Your English is excellent, are you on holiday here?" she was curious.

"Long story," he replied. "I came with Devlin, I don't know how long we will be here," as he spoke he sounded sad, and she picked up on the mood.

"Do you ride?" Daisy asked cheerfully, changing the subject unconsciously trying to lift his mood, and he looked surprised at the question.

"I do ride, but not for a while. My parents have horses, I grew up around them. It's in the blood you know - us Spanish," he laughed, and it was not lost on him that it was for the first time in a few weeks he had even felt like a smile, let alone a laugh.

"Come on, I have something to show you," she held out her hand and took his, leading him away from the garden into the paddock at the side of the house. She excused herself from Megan and Ruth who grinned at her and took the hint that she wanted this new attractive man to herself. Since they moved into the Old Mill House, her father Alex had built stables and Daisy now owned three horses. Another way to spend the money that was taken from the heist. More money laundering. Daisy, of course knew nothing of this, but just thanked her doting father for spoiling her.

They wandered around the stables chatting and patting the noses of the magnificent animals. Daisy was pleased to have another human being who loved them as much as she did. Jess was ok around them, but she wasn't a 'horsey' person, and neither was Alex really. Even Ruth and Megan had no interest in horses, so she was thrilled to find another person that took an interest in her passion.

"Come round tomorrow, early, and we can take them out around the lanes if you have nothing on?" Daisy came right out with the invitation, but Dom was reluctant to accept the offer. He said he would need to speak to Devlin first, see what he thought. This was no time for stepping on his toes and upsetting him, he was not going to convey that information to Daisy, she would think he was weak if he did.

"Erm, ok, I don't think we have anything on tomorrow. Give me your number and I'll confirm one way or another, I would love that, to get out and see a bit of the island, thank you," he sounded unsure, like a little boy. So Daisy was left with neither a yes or a no. He kissed her hand when he said goodnight to her. A gesture that sent shivers down her spine. He kept on showing her the traits of a man with some class, a good upbringing, a gentleman.

She relayed their conversation about the ride to Alex when they had all left later that evening.

"It was very strange, as if Devlin has some kind of hold over him, he couldn't agree to come over for a ride without his permission!" She was quite bemused and confused.

"How old is he? thirty-ish, must be. Odd reason for somebody his age, having to ask to go out to play," he laughed. "I was curious myself. Strange bunch, wonder what they are up to, only time will tell," Alex was also now more than interested and suspicious of the new gathering next door.

"Small world eh?" Jamal was asking Devlin about Alex.

"Indeed it is, you know him? Asked Devlin…"

"Our paths have crossed, we met in the Paris office years ago, I don't know how he thinks or where his loyalties lie really, he isn't adverse to turning a blind eye if the price is right. We were wise not to say too much, I liked her, Jess? And the daughter, but him… he has something of authority about him, I can smell it at a hundred paces, might be trouble…" He was thoughtful and careful with his words as he spoke.

"Really? That IS interesting! A blind eye, I will remember that. I will find out whose side he is on," Devlin agreed they needed to know. He would ask Maria, she would know something about him.

Daisy McFarlane could not sleep. It had been a while since she let anybody stir her emotions and this man tonight had certainly dipped his mysterious charms into her empty heart. He was so good to look at and there was something harmless and intriguing about him. Not like the usual people she mixed with at University, he had a worldly air about him. She needed to find out more and when she eventually drifted off to sleep it was to dream of him in another landscape, Spain, with the horses and the desert and the sunshine. She woke with a start as Jess came into her room, throwing open her curtains, to tell her he was in fact downstairs and responding to her invitation to an early ride on the horses!"

"Perfect," she moaned as Jess strung back the curtains on rope ties, revealing another glorious Isle of Wight day, with air so crisp and clear, if you could bottle it there was a fortune to be made.

"Tell him, no ask him, to wait I won't be long." She shot out of bed and jumped in the shower, pulling on riding gear and ran down the stairs to see him sitting with Jess at the kitchen table. He looked comfortable chatting to her, not like the awkward man she had spoken to yesterday. He was laughing and he threw his head back as he responded to one of Jess's comments. A very different Dom to the one in Devlin's company. He was just gorgeous to look at, not unlike her Dad, dark and swarthy, a good body and a beautiful smile. His face lit up when he smiled. She wanted to see that smile even more today. He seemed bigger today, bigger than the shadow she saw in her garden when he was with Devlin and those French blokes. It was obvious he was under some kind of spell… she stopped herself – SPELL? What are you 14 years old? She laughed to herself and went into the kitchen. He stood up when she entered the room, she was somehow not surprised he did this, it was not often a man stands up, when a woman comes into the room. Certainly not the men she knew, one Brownie point to him. Another tick in the box.

She grabbed a quick orange juice and took Dom out to the paddock, found him a riding hat that he refused and a crop that he accepted. After helping her onto her horse like a true gentleman he jumped on the back of her favourite horse. He was agile and natural with them, knowing exactly what he was doing. They rode out for what seemed like hours, through the village, up through Knighton, over the fields and stopped at the top of Brading Downs to admire the view. He was overwhelmed by the island, mainly because it seemed deserted and so green, he was transfixed by the thatched cottages they encountered along the route, they could see for miles from that vantage point on top of the Downs; he told Jess he had never been there before, in fact he had never been to England. Commenting that he loved Island life he said he had been born on an island. She asked which one, but he changed the subject cleverly and quickly by saying it wasn't as beautiful as this one, leaving her without an answer. They chatted like old friends, but she wanted to find out about him so kept the conversation as light as she could. She didn't have to work hard with him, he was ready to chat about certain things but not his background it seemed.

"It is so good to be out of that house, I am suffocating in there with Devlin and this new chap that has arrived Jamal and his son. I am not sure I like either of them very much, not sure what they are up to but it's intense. The phone is going all day long and I don't know what is going on up there, they are planning something, and I have no part in any of it. I want to go home but can't see that happening any time soon," he looked sad as he spoke.

"What are they planning ? Why aren't you going home?" Daisy was curious. If he wanted to go home he should go home. It seemed obvious that he was being held against his will, but that didn't make sense as he was out here with her, and he could leave at any time. She was oblivious to the fact he had no passport and no money, but he wasn't ready to tell her that. Maybe when he got to know her he could confide in her and ask for help. He had thought about telephoning his father, but Devlin watched him like a hawk and there was never an opportune moment to use the telephone. Even if he did speak to his father he was afraid of the consequences of bringing such shame on his family, so he thought he would bide his time until the perfect moment to escape emerged.

"I don't know what they are planning but I have to be here, it's a long story and one I can't share right now, sorry," he apologised.

"Ok, well if you ever want to talk about it I'm a good listener, comes with the job!" she laughed, it was the only thing she could think to say to him. He didn't pick up on her comment about her job. It was baffling and she could not stop thinking about the reasons he was here but didn't want to be. Was he working? Was he being paid to stay? Did one of the others have some kind of hold over him?, It didn't make sense. She would find out, give it time.

CHAPTER 9

The Russian and Maria arrived at The Copse on the same day, it was chaos. Maria didn't tell anybody, and after waiting twenty four hours for the release papers to be issued following her successful Parole appeal, she was on her way. She was freed early with some restrictions regarding travel, but she was happy with anything that would get her out of there.

When she arrived in the morning it was a shock to them all. They had all got into a routine of sorts and she broke that routine as soon as she set foot inside her new glass palace.

It was her house, and understandably, as soon as she saw the wonderful view from the master bedroom with the glass balcony she assumed that was her room, a silent announcement, by just putting her bag onto the bed in that room.

Devlin stepped in immediately and said no. Reasoning with her was pointless, he tried that, but it became a huge row. He stood his ground and refused to move the desks and explained the extra phone lines were in that room and it was perfect for the office. They all needed light, air, and a view so this was the room. The office space designated for the house was dingy and on the ground floor, almost sunk into the ground like a cellar with a short flight of stone steps into it. There was no way he was going to use that or rethink the office space that he had set up in there, so reluctantly and with a great deal of shouting and stamping of feet, she backed down, taking the room next door and slamming the door as she went in. It had the same view, but no glass balcony so this was very much a compromise from her…for now.

Smiling with a great deal of satisfaction at this outcome he was glad he did that, knowing he needed to show some strength in front of her, start as you mean to go on… she was seething but inside so glad to be out of prison she threw herself onto her bed and sobbed silently, with shock but mainly relief to be free.

He was angry with her, things were running smoothly, and she was trying to throw a big spanner in the works within minutes of arrival.

The stockily built Russian with the wild hair, reminded Devlin of Rasputin with his long beard and long grey and black hair that seemed to be in even stripes, he was tall, with broad shoulders and looked formidable. He arrived later in the day and all that was missing was a fanfare of golden trumpets as he got out of the taxi, his blue brocade jacket catching the evening sun, the gold thread running through it glinting as he strode up the path and banged on the door.

He stomped all over the house demanding everything they did not have, a certain coffee, black bread, a room with a view… it went on until Devlin spoke to him and negotiated a deal that shut him up. Despite his grand blustery entrance and demands, Devlin liked him straight away and put him into the team in his head. Just what we need, some presence and strength. He was so glad he was a hundred times removed from Matt in looks, personality, just so refreshingly different which was a bonus.

He arrived, they shook hands, they spoke, and it was a done deal. There was no room for if's or maybe's he was in. Jamal was gloating with 'I told you so's,' and said 'I knew you would like him' so many times, Devlin had to tell him to shut up. There was no way this Russian was going to be turned down to be part of this team. Devlin had been railroaded into accepting him but despite that he felt he would be an asset if he didn't step out of line too much. Only time would tell, a risk he needed to take.

Dom tried to stay out of it, but he was getting increasingly restless watching the feverish activity and only catching every other word. They seemed to argue a lot, vying for position, that was clear, and now Maria was back, that awful woman, he described her to Daisy and Jess; he was spending more and more time with Daisy at the Old Mill House. Devlin didn't seem to notice his absence which suited him. He needed to get away from them, he had no place there, but the hold Devlin had over him was huge and he was terrified he would be held to account for the loss of Ria on the boat. Every time he returned from seeing Daisy, Devlin questioned him to confirm he had kept his mouth shut and reminded him to keep it shut, every time Dominic agreed.

Eventually Maria got time alone with Devlin who was more than attentive, but forcing pleasantries with her, he really loathed this woman, there was nothing about her he liked...except her house of course and a hidden fortune. His acting skill was so convincing – Oscar worthy, she actually thought he was interested in her and she perked up no end. The old Maria was emerging, matching clothes and lots of makeup made an appearance on the second day back, much to the surprise and amusement of all the men in the house. She overdid it somewhat but none of them said anything. Devlin had put a few things in her wardrobe and guessed at colour and styles. When he saw her he came to the conclusion maybe she would have to go and do her own shopping…

The lift in her mood however crashed dramatically when she realised they had all been next door to socialise with Jess and Alex McFarlane. Maria reminded Devlin who he was – MI6 and probably could be responsible for ending the Chale Bay drop in 1969. Devlin told her he was aware but relayed Jamal's thoughts that although this 'enemy' was too close for comfort, he may have a foot in both camps if the price was right. It gave both of them lots to think about. Maybe using The Copse as their HQ wasn't such a good idea… they would have to discuss it when they had all settled in. But then again, right under his nose? It seemed perfect. In plain sight was the phrase that kept occurring to Devlin. It would be too obvious but not obvious at all.

One major problem, no two major problems occurred to Devlin. As quickly as he solved one problem, another popped into his head. Number one was Dominic, that problem had been there since they arrived, well before they arrived, but now he was mixing with Daisy and her family. If he suddenly disappeared they would notice. Maybe he had waited too long to deal with him. It needed more careful thought, number two problem, the boat and now there was a third, which might be Alex McFarlane. Jamal recognised him, and he was uncomfortably close. Maybe they needed a cover story. Maria and Matt operated under a legitimate Procurement Company, this new venture had nothing to hide behind. This needed some thought and maybe some action. Alex was pleasant enough but if he was still involved with MI5 or MI6, and he didn't know the difference if he was honest with himself, then they needed to be very careful or deal with him and that wouldn't be difficult. Keep your friends close and your enemies closer, isn't that an old saying? He wasn't sure but it fit this situation. He would certainly do his best. Organising this he was discovering more and more problems daily, it was like juggling mice, you start with two and end up with dozens.

CHAPTER 10

In Palma, Mallorca, the Montpelier family were distraught. Their only son Dominic was missing and so was his friend Devlin and the family yacht. They disappeared on the same night and there had been no sighting of the boat and no word from either men since. Dominic had never taken the boat out on his own before, and they were praying that he had taken it, because if somebody they didn't know had taken him and the boat that was too awful to contemplate, but that didn't explain Devlin's apparent disappearance.

The local police were involved, and they quickly found the note scribbled in their apartment which said **'away for a few days, don't worry D**.' Devlin Marshall was also missing but the note seemed to say only one of them was going away, they had no idea who had written the note – Dominic or Devlin. It had confused them all. They hoped that is was just a whim or a prank and they had both taken off for some kind of adventure, but it was so uncharacteristic of either of them to just disappear without a call or a proper note. The beach business remained closed, so they had not made contingency plans for that deepening concern.

They realised that the friendship between them was volatile, they had seen too many rows between them, and they knew very little about Devlin, except he and their only son had the beach business and shared an apartment where Dominic stayed most of the time, in the centre of Palma. In fact they knew nothing about Devlin but had no reason to think or worry that he had done anything to harm Dom. There was no ransom demanded and not one clue as to the whereabouts of either son, boat or Devlin. They did not care about the boat, but they did care that their son had been missing for several weeks now which was so out of character. The alarm was raised after three days and police on the island were searching and making enquiries. Interpol had been informed and partygoers questioned. There were no real answers. Nobody saw them outside of the party that night or since. The family hired a private investigator who was drawing as many blanks as the police, but they were determined to find out where Dominic was and bring him home.

The only clue to his disappearance was a girl called Rebecca. Apparently Dominic was with her at a party on the night he disappeared, she had not been seen since that night either. Nobody seemed to know this girl, apart from her name and they had been seen together at other people's houses, so they were no further forward.

All the hospitals had been contacted and eventually a girl

matching her description was found in hospital in Palma, they believe having fallen overboard on the night that Dom went missing. A miracle survival they were saying in the town, this young woman who was found clinging to a life belt and picked up by a fishing boat, could not remember much due to the shock and the injury to her face. She kept saying Becca , so they were hoping that was her own name, with an English accent, they did not believe she was a local girl, nobody had been reported missing and so she was a mystery, but too much of a coincidence not to be connected to their son. They were not allowed to see her as the police were conducting their own investigations.

She had severe concussion but was doing well and lucky to be alive. They had no idea how she ended up in the middle of the ocean in the middle of the night, naked and injured. Police were interviewing her almost daily trying to establish her identity, but progress was slow, and recollection of what happened to her almost non-existent. The medical staff insisted it was the shock and her memory would probably come back in time.

Devlin was thinking about the boat and Dom and what to do with both. At some point he knew his family would be missing him as they were a close knit bunch. The boat was more of a problem, moored in full sight in Bembridge on the island, it was only a matter of time before somebody spotted it as stolen, so he needed a plan to get rid of it. It was too risky to attempt to sell it, but he might try. He was doubtful he could trust Dominic to go home and keep his mouth shut so that was something he would discuss with Maria. He would be charged with murder, and he kept reminding Dom of this when the conversation came around to him going home as it did almost daily now.

Dom was overtaking the boat as the prime problem, he was now missing from The Copse. Devlin went to find him just after lunch, three days after Maria and the Russian turned up on the same day. Since their arrival the last few days had been manic, with arguing and heated discussion about tactics and personal position within the new Organisation, he had so much to do and so much to think about he took his eye off the Dominic ball, his heart sunk when he suddenly realised he hadn't seen him for more than twenty four hours. Devlin panicked.

Dominic and Daisy were together, in Cowes, in her apartment overlooking the Solent. The sun was sparkling on the grey blue sea and the sunlight streaming across the vast array of colourful sails in the harbour was giving them even more vibrant colour as the boats beneath the sails bobbed up and down on the gentle waves in the bay.

The sun was also sharing its rays with them on their balcony, they stood hand in hand looking as if they were in the spotlight on a stage in the theatre. They loved watching the ferries, cruise ships and small boats, sail past, relieved and glad to have escaped parents and the mayhem of The Copse. It had not taken them long to realise there was a strong attraction between them having spent every minute they could together since they met, it became obvious that they had a lot in common, the horses, being outdoors; they were on the same wavelength and since the first ride up to Brading Downs could not keep their hands off each other.

That first time they took the horses out, the day after the garden party at the Old Mill House, they tied the horses up on a gorse bush and lay on the grass looking at the scenery and the blue sky that looked like a watercolour in a gallery, their first kiss was like electricity between them, and the passion between them was real. They lay there in the sunshine exploring each other for a long time. A falling in love moment for both of them, but with no words. Just that overwhelming feeling you are granted, by that invisible force, when that perfect person comes into your life. He was gentle and a perfect gentleman, she looked at him and was stunned at how much she was attracted to him. It was ridiculously quick, she only met him yesterday, but she had suffered many silly boyfriends in her group at University and none of them made her feel like he did after just a few hours.

Perhaps it was the fresh air or the need to grow up or just plain chemistry, but she wanted him and would fight for him whatever he had done, she felt there was something he wasn't telling her because it would shock her. She wanted to say – I know how you feel, whatever it is I can offer some empathy here. I have been where you are now. It felt like the secret of the shooting when she was 14, she never spoke about it to her friends in case they thought badly of her. A man killed right in front of her, in her house. She blocked it out and told none of her close friends. Until the court case nobody outside her immediate family knew about it. She hoped it was not as serious as that but only time would tell.

He was mysterious in his way, most men don't treat women the way he did, and she knew it was borne from something special, and she wanted to know more.

Dom was clearly unhappy living at The Copse and although she had no idea why, and would wait for him to tell her, getting him away from there seemed the perfect solution. He was like a different person out of The Copse and the company up there. She had this apartment standing empty for most of the time; she loved being at The Old Mill House with her father and Jess, but if she was honest with herself, she was tired of playing the child. Time to move into the Cowes apartment and on a whim and a gut feeling, offered the refuge to Dom. She said nothing to Jess or Alex who would probably not approve of the gesture to a complete stranger. They were very protective, but she was twenty five years old and too old to ask permission from parents. He did not hesitate and was emotional when she told him she had somewhere they could go. It was as if an enormous weight had been lifted off his shoulders. He was in the depths of despair and couldn't see a way out. This was like a dream, a miracle revelation that she had an apartment, and he could go there. Away from Devlin Marshall and that house.

"Daisy are you sure?" he was beside himself with gratitude at that moment. "I will repay you one day for your kindness, you are a very special girl," he promised and looked at her intensely. Not believing he had found this gentle, kind, beautiful English girl who was not at all what he had come to expect. He had met many

English girls in his job on the beach and Daisy was not like the exuberant holidaymakers he met, fuelled with alcohol and not really showing their true selves in a strange country, with all inhibitions out of the window for two weeks, when they seemed to leave all their gentle traits at home!

"Look, I am not going to ask right now, but I get the feeling you don't want to be at The Copse," she knew the answer before he replied.

"It's so complicated, and I can't explain. I will one day. You are such a wonderful girl Daisy, I am lucky to have found you, but PLEASE don't tell anybody where I am, please, my life might depend on it," he kissed her on her cheek and hugged her like a sister. She was so pleased to be able to help him and promised not to divulge their secret. She caught his comment about his life depending on it, so knew this was probably serious, but what she could not imagine.

"Of course I won't unless you want me to. Nobody comes here unless I ask them to, you are very welcome, just promise me you will tell me something soon? If I don't know then I can't help." She left it at that.

Devlin decided it was time to do something about Dom, he didn't trust him to keep his mouth shut and he was not going to risk the rest of his life for one slip of the tongue. If Daisy and her family missed him he could make up some excuse. He made some calls.

Dom had nothing to collect from The Copse, he only had the clothes he stood up in and a couple of shirts and some underwear Devlin had given him to tide him over until they decided what to do next. There was no point going back there but he had forgotten his wallet with his worldly possessions inside. She did not ask what was inside, but it was a picture of his parents and his little sister Nicole that he wanted to keep with him. Daisy dropped him at the bottom of the lane, making sure there were no cars coming in either direction so they wouldn't be seen. She then drove on to the Old Mill House, not wanting to risk anybody seeing them together. He told her he would walk back to the Old Mill House, and they could go back to Cowes together. Two minutes later he walked into The Copse to a hail of questions.

"Where have you been? Devlin is going mad looking for you," Jamal was first with the tirade. It was like school, as if he was a schoolboy playing truant. Evan Theo chipped in,

"You are in trouble, Devlin is mad as hell," he scoffed at Dom, even his own father would not speak to him like that. Dom ignored him and ran upstairs to find his wallet. On the way back down the stairs he heard them talking and stopped dead in his tracks to listen to their conversation.

"I don't think Devlin wants him here, wonder who he is and why he is here. I heard Devlin say get rid of him," Theo was speaking to Jamal.

"Surely not, you must be mistaken," Jamal sounded shocked. "He seems harmless enough, but I agree he is a spare part here," they stopped talking. Jamal gestured towards the stairs and put a finger up at his mouth as if to warn his son to be quiet in case Dom heard them. But it was too late.

"No, I heard him on the phone yesterday, that's why he is mad he couldn't find him. He told whoever he was speaking to – be here today and keep a look out. Find him."

Dom froze and went back up the stairs. He opened the door to the balcony room and looked around, moving papers on the desk. He wasn't even sure what he was looking for but, something, anything to give him clues to how Devlin was thinking. He opened a drawer and saw a small pistol under some papers, just a small piece of metal but he recognised the shape, moved the paperwork and picked it up, putting it in his pocket. His heart was beating fast as he tucked it away. As he left the balcony bedroom he looked through the side window on the landing and saw a car sitting in the lane, it looked like a Daimler, black with dark windows. It was so unusual to see any car drive down the lane let alone be parked and it caught his attention straight away. It felt weird to think he suspected Devlin of wanting to get rid of him, but for weeks now he had been feeling that he was not safe here. Maybe he wants me dead. End of his problem. Time to go. If he walked down the lane he would be seen, time for a new plan.

Devlin and Maria were out, and it looked as if they had taken Devlin's car. Maria's MGB was parked by the side of the house, and he knew where the keys were. She was pedantic about hanging keys were she could find them, it had something to do with the fire; she said something about 'a place for everything, and everything in its place' saved my life. Maybe these keys would save his life. He crept down the side stairs that led out to the garage and the rooms under the main house. They were meant to be a utility room and office, but just used for storage.   As he hoped the keys to the MGB were on the hook and he took them, opening the side door and getting into the canary yellow car. He could hardly slip out unseen in this car with such a distinctive colour, but he had no choice. It was parked facing out so he could make a fast run down to the gate and go in the opposite direction to the Daimler that was waiting, so obviously, watching the house.   Nobody parked there ever, it was a private road so only residents and delivery people came down the lane, it was so conspicuous it was funny.   Dom wasn't laughing though, and his heart was beating as fast as bees wings as he put the clutch in, rammed the MG into first gear, and pulled away without making a sound on the driveway. This was no time for screeching tyres or scattering gravel.   Time to put into action the practise he had with all the high powered cars on his family estate.   He didn't know the island very well but knew he could probably find his way back to Cowes and give these morons the slip whoever they were.   After hearing the conversation inside the house about Devlin wanting to get rid of him he felt certain they were looking for him.   He would deal with Devlin at some point. He was away and up the hill, going towards Newchurch, through the narrow lanes that were empty. He was glad it was rural and not the town so he could get some distance between them. It took some guts to drive at any speed down those narrow lanes, if something came towards him he would be in trouble. They were sure to follow him if they spotted him pulling out of the driveway. Wasting no time he got to the crossroads at Newchurch, and had a dilemma, do I turn right to Newport or left to Sandown?

He needed to get to Cowes without them catching him. He had no idea why he turned left and found himself heading for Sandown, right would have taken him to Newport and then Cowes but he didn't know that. As he got to the T junction at Lake he saw the Daimler in his rear view mirror, some distance away but there they were. He was right, they were after him. Suddenly a tractor pulled out in front of him, and his heart missed a beat, he had encountered these vehicles before on English roads, travelling at the speed of snails, and on such narrow roads he would be trapped, so without thinking he took a quick look in his mirror and pulled out; there was a huge green lorry coming towards him, but he was a good driver, and he swerved right in front of the tractor and avoided the lorry by millimetres. The lorry sounded his horn, a long blast from a very hacked off driver. The tractor might give him a few minutes to get clear of the Daimler.

The colour of the car he was driving was too bright to blend into the background and he couldn't help thinking Maria could not have chosen a more visible colour for her car, so he needed to put some distance between them and fast. He had no idea how to do a detour and lose them, so he ploughed on up the main route. The lights changed and he screamed up the hill in Lake and over the bridge heading towards Arthurs Hill and Shanklin. Just pulling into Shanklin he saw them, they were still behind him, quite a few cars between them but they were there, one glance at the fuel gauge told him he was good for a few miles, so he put his foot down, dipping down into Shanklin Old Village flying past pretty thatched cottages, including the 'Crab Inn' racing up the hill towards Luccombe, the road was wide and empty, round a couple of tight bends, the little sportscar hugged the road, he could see open road in front of him, winding around the spectacular green hillside, this was it. Time to put some miles between them, he was doing over 80 when he dropped into Ventnor that had hills as steep as anything he ever saw in his home country.

For a minute or so he lost the Daimler and roared away, Whitwell was on the sign, so he turned a sharp right and up an even steeper part of the hill. It felt like the side of a mountain it was so steep. He decided to do a u turn and go back down the same way he had just come thinking he did not want to keep on climbing. Time to lose them, there was no way he was going to continue up this massively steep hill, concerned the clutch on the MG just would not handle it, so a quick flick of his wrist and he had whipped the MG around and was heading back down towards the sharp bends of Ventnor.

He shot past them coming up towards him on the steepest part of the road, it was a 'T' junction almost at the top of the hill, there was no way they would be able to flip around as he had done. Their clumsy, heavy Daimler would struggle to do the same on such a steep hill giving him more precious time to get away. There they were…two men wearing sunglasses. He heard the brakes of the Daimler and then the crash as they hit the wall. They had tried to turn to follow him and clipped a kerb… The steep gradient of the hill naturally tipped the weight of the Daimler and the car rolled over and over down the hill smashing it as it if were a toy under an elephants foot. As it hit a stone wall halfway down, the car catapulted and flew into the air and over the wall rolling until it hit another wall; one of the petrol tanks blew and the car exploded as it continued its path down the hillside, hitting trees and bollards the other fuel tank exploded and what was left of the car continued to bounce and scatter over rocky ledges. The wreckage of the Daimler smashed beyond recognition, came to rest in flames against the wall of a hotel on the main road.

Dom kept on driving as fast as the MG would go, right foot flat on the floor, no time for stopping to see if they are ok. He knew they could not survive that. And he was right, both men, he assumed hired by Devlin, were dead.   Dom headed back the way he had come, looking for a road sign for Cowes thinking about his family. He made up his mind to ring his father deciding that his wrath and disappointment could not be worse than this. If Devlin was determined he would be dead too and very soon. What a b*stard he thought. Ten years of my life and he wants me dead. Well Mr Devlin Marshall, I am not listening to you any more, I am out of here.   The shock of the incident on the boat had now reached a point, where the fog and horror in his head was clearing, and he could at last think with some clarity.   He would face the music if he had to, come clean. He didn't kill that girl deliberately, he wanted to stop, and Devlin refused.   The threats from Devlin had prevented him coming forward and telling what really happened. He needed to clear his name if he was to have any kind of life, he hoped that life would include Daisy, she deserved the truth and the best of everything. She had no idea of the wonderful life he could offer her, he wanted to give her the world. His world that was privileged with money, a wonderful family who had love to spare, a very good life indeed. She could live in luxury for the rest of her life with him if that is what she wanted, and he wanted her. His heart was bursting with love for her, but they could not live like this.

He abandoned Maria's car in Newport in an empty side street, leaving the keys in the ignition. He saw the sign for Cowes knowing if he took the car all the way to Daisy's then he was leaving clues to his location, and he wasn't going to put her in that kind of danger. He would get a taxi or a bus to Cowes from Newport. It was at this point he realised there were two places called Cowes, East Cowes and West Cowes and he had no idea where Daisy's apartment was or the name of the road, it was on the seafront, so he took a gamble with the taxi. He would recognise it once he got there asking the driver him to drop him on the sea front at East Cowes. Luckily, there was a ferry to take him to West Cowes. An easy mistake.

As he walked the rest of the way to Daisy's apartment a thought struck him, something that had not occurred to him until that moment. He was driving Maria's car. How did those people know it was him driving? Were they thinking it was Maria? He had long dark hair just like her. Was it Maria they were after? If it was, then this was not over for him or her. He needed to lay low and get in touch with his family and get out of here. One thing he did know, he was in dangerous company, his life was in danger, maybe Maria's life was in danger. It was like living in a movie, and he wanted no part of it.

Chapter 11

Alex McFarlane was on his way to Palma, Mallorca. One of his team, Rebecca Nelson went missing whilst working under cover a few weeks ago. She was getting close to Devlin Marshall and the last message from her indicated she had befriended one of his friends, a very close friend in fact, his business partner Dominic Montpelier.

Alex got word that a young woman answering her description was in a hospital in Palma. She was talking about 'Becca' and about a boat trip and being police, but she was so confused they thought she wanted to speak to the police. One of the young policemen who went to the hospital to speak to her was informed that a private detective had been enquiring about a missing girl and two missing men, he put two and two together and Alex eventually got the message that she might be the same Rebecca that was missing from his department. Only time would tell, but it would be strange if she was not the same undercover agent they sent to Palma.

It had been weeks since she checked in and nobody had seen or heard from her, so he was hopeful the pieces would fit, and answers would be forthcoming soon. What he found was very different from his expectations. It was Rebecca but she had no idea who he was. The doctors said it would take time for her memory to return and she had only very sketchy recollection of what had happened to her. Due to the shock they thought it may be weeks or months, or she could just recover quickly; this kind of recovery was a lottery. She was getting the best care.   Alex wanted to talk to her just to see if she could remember anything.

"Rebecca ?" he spoke gently to her, and she looked at him. She had a vacant look about her and her eyes seemed dull and unresponsive, he didn't know her well, but this was not the vibrant girl he remembered, the doctors told him she had been in the water for several hours before they found her. She was lucky to be alive after the exposure and the shock of falling overboard. Well that was what they were surmising. She had an injury to her face which could have happened when she fell overboard, or it explained why she fell from the boat. They were listening to her and trying to piece it together slowly but not much of it made sense.

She looked up at him and smiled, not a recognition smile, but just a pleasant hello smile, she said one word, "Sorry."

"No need to say sorry, why are you sorry?" for a second Alex had a hopeful moment, that she knew something.

"Sorry I can't remember anything, except water and Dom, and I don't know what Dom is? Just stupid," she lowered her head and he helped her.

"Dom is a person," a man that you were with on a boat," he had to tell her but not in a pushy way, just gently introduce the idea.

"Is it? Dom a person, and my face?" she touched her face

that was bruised. "I remember a man, a tall man who shouldn't have been there, they found me, they found me," she was crying.

A nurse came in and said enough for today.

Alex left his card on her table and Rebecca looked at it and touched it. His number was on the card, and he just said "Ring me if you remember anything. I'll come back tomorrow and see you. Is there anything you need?"

She shook her head and then as he was leaving the room she called him back.

"Find Dom, just find Dom, I think Dom will help me."

Alex was aware that Dom must be the man that came to his own house with Devlin Marshall. Of course it is the same person, too much of a coincidence for it to be anybody else. How many Dom's could there be connected to Devlin Marshall? His Department had sent Rebecca Nelson to Palma after a tip off that he was there working on the beach with a young local man. It had taken them the best part of nine years to track him down and she had volunteered to go and get close to them both. She nearly paid with her life which was shocking. He needed to get to the bottom of it. Was it an accident? Did they push her overboard? Did they find out who she was? Too many unanswered questions, and why did they leave her and not alert the coastguard?

And why was Devlin now back in the UK thinking he could wipe his slate clean? There was not much evidence to link him with the Chale Beach drugs haul, but he was friends with Maria and Matt and now he was he back on the island living in her house, why? Previous crime he was involved in might hold water, trouble is they had very little evidence to link him with any of it. He needed to bide his time and find out more.

This new clue, Rebecca miraculously surviving her ordeal, was the first step. He was aware that his own daughter Daisy had become friends with Dom, and it made alarm bells ring. Was she safe with him? Was he capable of murder? Because if Ria had died then that would have been the outcome. He went cold just thinking about it. He needed to act fast but what to do next. His instinct was to wait there for another day and try and speak to Ria again, and maybe speak to Dominic's parents. That idea had not occurred to him until this minute. He would contact the police department and find them.

He needed Jess to go and talk to Maria, he knew she was not keen to do that, but she might get some idea from Devlin or Maria what they were up to. He would see Ria tomorrow and get Daisy away from Dom whatever that took, he too might have to go into hiding with Jess. Having Devlin Marshall next door and this Dominic Montpelier who was capable of… well what was he capable of? Attempted murder? He would take no chances.

Alex had property that he could go to on the island, property that nobody knew about. He had been clever enough to create a new identity to purchase them through a third party to launder the money he took from the gang who organised the Chale Bay drugs heist.   He could operate from there and continue to investigate why there was now new activity at The Copse. What were they up to? He would need to find out, he should put people in place to do just that and it was only a matter of time before he would be forced to, but for now he was hanging on to certain information.

Alex arranged for a permanent female guard to be put on the hospital room, it was the only way he could keep her safe. He had no idea if she was in danger but could take no chances. He could not stay there indefinitely waiting for her to recover and his own family needed him to protect them.   He stayed for three more days and visited Rebecca every day.

Day three however it was a very different story from Rebecca , back at the hospital, she told Alex she felt safe with Gabriella looking after her, just knowing she was by her door made her feel more relaxed. Her face was still very bruised and had changed colour as bruises do in time, and she smiled when Alex arrived.

"Hello Alex, I am so glad you are still here, I was afraid you had gone back to England before I told you I had remembered something," she patted the bed and invited him to sit down.

"Good morning, you look a bit better today, anything you remember will help piece things together.   I have to go back to England today, but Gabriella will stay with you until they say you can be released. I want you to come back to England, your family are

worried and will look after you. Do you remember your family?"
Alex waited for her reply and was surprised at her recollections.

"My family, I had not thought about my family, but yes I
think I remember, but that is not what my brain is trying to say. Not
family but Dom, I remember Dom. I have been seeing him for a
while now, we went to lots of parties, and we went to his father's
boat after a party. Dom left me and I heard men shouting, I went
up on deck and Dom was arguing with a man. I think it was his
business partner,   next thing I remember was a pain in my face and
hitting the water. I don't think he saw me..." she stopped.

"What do you mean he didn't see you?" this was important,
what did she mean?

"I was behind Dom, his arm hit me, but it was an accident,
he didn't see me behind him. I am so stupid."

"Why was he on the boat? His business partner" Alex asked
the obvious question.

"I don't know, I remember Dom being shocked the boat was
moving and he went up to the deck to find out."

"What? He had taken the boat out? Do you think he was
stealing the boat?" Alex asked her, but she wouldn't know that...the
thought of course had occurred to him over the weeks. That was
it... Devlin was stealing the boat.   His mind was racing, he steals
the boat, Dom and Ria were on board, but he had no idea, they

argue, she gets in the middle of it and nearly dies. Seemed too easy to piece together. Could it be so simple? How else would Devlin get back to England. He was wanted by Interpol and could not go through customs at airports or ferry ports without being spotted. So where was the boat? On the island? It must be, what was Devlin up to? he needed to get back to England, but first there were people he needed to speak to.

The next day, with the address of the Montpelier's in his pocket he arrived at the gates of their home. It took his breath away, nestled on a hill side with spectacular views over the countryside he knew there was some status here. This was not the home of an ordinary Spanish family, he found himself confronted by armed guards on the entrance and some checking of his I.D. before he was allowed to go through the gates. Enormous iron gates festooned with lions and the coat of arms of the family? He was surprised to say the least.

He was greeted by Dominic's mother, she introduced herself as Marta and apologised for her husband's absence, explaining that he would join them shortly. She led Alex out to the back of the house and for the second time that day he held his breath at the vastness and beauty of the garden and the view in front of him. He found himself saying "Wow," out loud, and Marta laughed.

"Yes it is wonderful, we are very lucky to live here. But please tell me about Dominic, is he safe, please tell me he is safe, why is he in England? We are beside ourselves with worry. We have had no word for weeks and weeks. It is not like him at all, he is such a good boy," she gestured to Alex to sit down on one of the many chairs on the balcony. The view was spectacular overlooking the mountains to the left and the azure blue sea that was some way down below them in the bay.

Alex had told them on the phone that Dom was alive and in England, so the visit and the information was not a complete surprise to her. A maid brought a tray adorned with some beautiful cups and saucers, plenty of cake cut into very neat squares and white napkins that looked freshly ironed with creases that would grace any five star hotel. Silver cutlery completed the display. It didn't take an expert in these things to recognise quality and class. He was confused about a man who would be involved with Devlin Marshall and be in a house on the Isle of Wight that was beautiful, but this was something else.

They were interrupted before Alex could explain about Dominic, he only had time to tell his mother that Dominic was indeed alive and in England, when François Montpelier appeared, tearing off his jacket and throwing it onto a chair. He shook Alex's hand with both of his, greeting him like an old friend and asked the same question, "Is our son safe, tell me please, I am going out of my mind, we are going out of our minds, and who are you by the way? Police?" he sat down and looked at Alex intently.

"He is safe dear, this kind man just told me our boy is safe," she patted his arm and he sat back as if with relief on hearing those words.

"But where the hell is he?" he demanded.

"Erm, yes police," he was not going to go into the MI5 MI6 business, it took too long to explain every time. "As I said to Mrs Montpelier when we spoke on the phone, he is in England, on a small island in the South called the Isle of Wight with Devlin Marshall," Alex told him.

"But why? And why haven't we heard from him, he never ever in all of his life walked away from us like this, is he in trouble? It is the only thing we can think of. He has done something, and he thinks we will be upset by it," he took a breath and wiped the sweat from his head. "Mr… erm Mr?"

"Alex, Alex McFarlane, just call me Alex please, I am part of the investigation into various things that I can't talk about right now, I don't believe your son in involved in any of it, but he has association with some of the people I am looking at. I can't say any more than that."

"I believe Devlin Marshall took your boat and your son and a girl called Rebecca Nelson were onboard. Marshall didn't know they were on the boat, and something happened, and the girl went overboard. I think your son and Devlin thought she was dead, but she survived. Devlin carried on to England, taking Dominic with him.

The parents looked at each other and grasped each other's hands as if to comfort each other. Then François Montpelier spoke.

"So this girl, how did she survive? Are you saying you think Dominic and Devlin thought she was dead and left her? Now they are hiding because they think they killed her?" He had put two and two together very quickly. A smart man thought Alex.

"Oh my God that is terrible, my son wouldn't do a thing like that," his mother was crying.

"Well that is exactly what I think happened. I think it was Dominic who hit her in the face, but I have spoken to her, and she seems to remember standing behind Dominic and he swung his arm back, seemingly to hit Devlin and it caught her face, knocking her out and overboard. Thankfully, she was picked up by a fishing boat, and is in a hospital in Palma.

"So it was an accident?" there was relief in François Montpelier's voice.

"Yes we think so, but Dominic doesn't know that and is maybe being held against his will by this Devlin Marshall to save himself, maybe they think they will both be up on a murder charge," Alex explained.

Well we never really liked him you know, strange fellow, full of himself, arrogant. In all the years they have been together in business, we know no more about him now than we did at the beginning. Secretive. We know nothing of his family or background, nothing. Good riddance I say. Right we need to get Dominic back here, how do we do that?"

"Well I can't help you with that I am afraid that is up to him, and your family what happens next. Before I go, do you have a picture of your boat? It may still be on the Isle of Wight, I would like to locate it. I can give you the address where he was staying but the rest is up to you, he may face some charges of leaving the scene of an accident but that is for the Spanish authorities not me," Alex concluded.

"Yes of course," they all got up and headed out towards the front door. They stopped at the door of the library and Mrs Montpelier took a family album down from a shelf then led Alex out along the vast hallway, laying the album on a side table, she chose a picture from one of the pages and gave it to Alex, a photo of the motor yacht…

Alex scribbled down the address of The Copse, said his goodbyes and left them holding hands on the steps of their beautiful home.

CHAPTER 12

The Russian was in South America, doing what he did best negotiating the future with groups of men that were as ruthless as he was and would be again if required. Well they hoped that was what he was doing. He arrived like a whirlwind to The Copse, and Maria was glad to be rid of him from the house when he finally said his goodbyes. They had endless meetings while he was there, planning their strategy into the early hours, the five of them, Devlin, Jamal, Theo, Nikolai and Maria. It was going to be a massive drop of drugs and weapons and the distribution from the island was going to be bigger than anything they had ever handled.

Maria had money from the insurance on the house, and the money she had taken from Matt, so she didn't need this. If Devlin had not appeared she would not have started all of this again, but there was no way she was going to let them do it without her and she felt the desire for some degree of control and power in the group when Devlin suggested they operated from somewhere else without her contribution; she was dragged in by her ego, which appealed to her even more than the money would bring her. It was what she had done for years enjoying the thrill and the danger of beating the system and selling at a huge profit. God help anybody who got in her way.

Devlin and Maria explained it all to Nikolai and reminded Jamal who had been taken out of the equation before the heist happened that last weekend in August 1969. It was clear there was a huge market for weapons now and Northern Ireland was one market they knew would be interested. Worldwide small arms, Kalashnikov rifles and ammunition were in great demand, so their focus of discussion was around having two shipments come in to Chale Bay, one from South America laden with drugs and the other from South Africa who were leading the world in arms manufacture.   Nikolai had Russian connections and he offered to conduct these negotiations as well as negotiating with the Cartels in New Mexico. With Jamal, his son, Maria and Devlin to back him up they had enough experience to crack this one without too much trouble. They were all confident about the major factors, it was just the finer detail that needed tweaking. Devlin was on top of all of that.

They had not decided 100% on the dropping point, but Chale Bay was looking like the obvious choice. It always was the best beach on a deserted part of the Isle of Wight with the best hidden cave to stash the goods temporarily when they were brought in by small boats.

They quickly came round to the idea of obtaining the goods from two continents and the major development that emerged from all the meetings at The Copse meant there were definitely going to be two oil tankers, one coming in from South America with the drugs and one from South Africa with the weapons, small arms, rifles, machine guns and ammunition.   It made sense to fill the tanker from New Mexico with drugs and not try and double up with small arms this

WIGHT DIAMONDS & CRAZY RED DOGS

time.

Chale Bay was still there, open and inviting them back in. Nothing had been closed and the cave was a natural feature of the cliff, to use it twice would be an outrageous cheek but one that may catch the authorities napping. Under discussion were the caves in Freshwater, including the one with the intriguing black door, just round the headland from Freshwater, as last time this cave was considered for backup storage, bearing in mind the size of the haul would probably be used this time.

Everything was changing in the UK, change of Government, a new woman Prime Minister and departments in Whitehall still being formulated so the time was right to strike while all this re-organising was taking place. There were so many strikes amongst official departments this was the ideal time to act while they vied for position in new roles in Parliament. Problems in Northern Ireland were filling the news and the Russians were infighting and Afghanistan was bubbling in the background. An unsettled time and perfect for catching the authorities napping.

Maria found The Russian sitting on his own, and spoke to him before he left, offering him contacts she remembered from El Paso but less than politely he refused, telling her in a fierce voice that he had his own contacts in Albuquerque and other places in New Mexico, reminding her that previous contacts may be less than happy to hear from them and particularly her, as the whole thing failed in 1969 with big losses for everybody. Despite this reminder and the response he got from her which was less than positive, he felt she would be trouble. Suffice to say they were suspicious of each other. There was no instant rapport that was obvious to all who heard them communicate. Because that was all it was between them communication, no real conversation. She tried to tell him things and he rejected her every word. This was not going well.

"You are a fool if you think those people will deal with you again, the world knows how you failed ten years ago. The world is still talking about your giant tanker failure, you are lucky I am here to give you some street credibility back!" his English was excellent, but the strong Russian accent and the tone and strength of his voice surprised and amused Maria. The comment about having street credibility was weird. What did he mean? Clearly ten years in prison had reduced her awareness of phrases. Part of her felt pleased he seemed fearless but at the same time, part of her was wary he was a force to be reckoned with.

"We will have to keep more than an eye on him Devlin, I'm not so sure he is the right man for this," she was concerned and said so as she poured another gin for herself. "Last night I heard him talking to himself in Russian!"

"Well right now we have little choice," replied Devlin, who also had his reservations, with alarm bells ringing when she mentioned him talking to himself...or was he talking to somebody else? The only convinced person in the house was Jamal who continued to compliment the Russian at every opportunity.

"Don't worry about him, he can look after himself and he will do a good job. He has his reasons for making this a success. He has the contacts, and he needs to make money to get his wife and children back with him, this is his moment, trust me," he was brimming with confidence as he spoke. He poured himself a drink and they all sat around discussing the next move.

Jamal did not mention the enemies that Nikolai Markarov seemed to attract and would always be circling; he made them wherever he went. Just his manner and tactics made him a target. He was on the most wanted list in Russia and escaped with his life more than once, getting his family out just in time, Jamal had helped him hide his family in Paris, so he was owed big time by the Russian. Nikolai was a man with a mission, and he would succeed, whatever it took, but he had huge problematic baggage in pursuit.

If Maria and Devlin took their eye off him for one second he would smash this Organisation into pieces and take what he felt he was owed. They had it coming, and he was an expert in double dealing … 'amateurs' was how he was thinking. But he had no idea what Maria was capable of, or indeed Jamal or Devlin.

Devlin was working his charm on Maria who still had her eyes firmly on him as more than business partner so he might allow himself to be sucked in, just for the rewards it might bring. He loved this house for starters, his selfish brain was in full swing. There could never be a romance, but could he fool her? The very thought sent him into a black hole of despair with a sick feeling in his stomach, but needs must, and he may be able to pull this one off – only time would tell. Maria had no idea about Martin Squire or the strange relationship he had shared with Dom for the best part of ten years that was definitely over and done with. She was getting more and more confident as the days slipped by and by the end of week two of her freedom she was strutting around in a familiar manner. She was not the attractive woman she once was, prison had not been kind to her and although she had lost weight in there, which suited her, her hair was not as thick and luxurious as it was before the sentence, and time had taken its toll on her skin. She started to use more and more makeup and knew she could not click her fingers at any man she wanted any more. Even Martin Squire had rejected her, she never understood that. She still found Devlin very attractive and told him so all those years ago, but he disappeared; nevertheless, here he was, and he had persisted in his efforts to see her in prison on a regular basis.

Pickings in the 'man' department were thin on the ground so she started to soften where Devlin was concerned. She had different reasons for a liaison than he did. She feared for her life, so security was high on her agenda, and he would be a good front man. Husband material? No she didn't think he would be interested in a million years, but he was giving her some signals that he might be interested so there was a tiny glimmer of hope.

He needed to get her away from The Copse to talk to her on her own. A weekend on the boat… that should do it. There would be a lull while the Russian worked his magic, and the last of the crew were hired so he took the opportunity to suggest a few days on their own to talk tactics.

Jamal and his very attractive son could hold the fort and continue building the team. Now there was a focus of interest for Devlin, Theo, he was a strange one. He didn't say much but his presence was felt. He was a huge fit young man with a body that was clearly in cahoots with at least one gym. He worked out in the garden each morning and Devlin watched him. He often caught Theo staring in his direction, they talked very little, but there was a chemistry between them, a tension, maybe sexual tension. This was not the time to test it, but they were drawn to each other no doubt about that.

His father always seemed to hold the conversations and he listened, intently, to everything. He had a laugh and smile that was intriguing, nothing seemed to bother him, and his body language was that of a confident and grounded individual, unlike Dom who seemed to have shrunk into his own shadow, so much so that he was currently nowhere to be found. Devlin was concerned about Dom who had not returned but he was guessing that Daisy had something to do with his disappearance. He would speak to her at some point and find out what was going on there, just to check Dom had kept his mouth shut about the accident on the boat. He could not risk that information leaking in her direction.

Chapter 13

"Darling Daisy, I have something I need to tell you," Dominic Montpelier was sitting on the side of her bed in the Cowes apartment. Another night of passion between them had made his head zing but not in the best way. He was finding the deceit of the last few months more than he could handle and had come to the decision to come clean. If he didn't tell somebody soon about what happened to Rebecca on his father's yacht he would literally go mad. How would she handle it ? He had no idea. He hated keeping this from her, and now this clear attempt to wipe him out with the car chase, it was all too much, and he needed his life back. Part of him believed he wasn't the target for the car chase, but he had to be careful now. If what he heard when he went back to The Copse was true then his life was in danger. He needed to keep away from Devlin for sure, for the first time in ten years he felt he couldn't trust him.

He had been missing from The Copse for over a week and he knew Devlin would be searching for him. He had no choice but to confide in her in the hope that she would believe that he had not meant to kill Ria and maybe, if he was lucky, she would help him return home to his family. It was a mess, but he was praying she would understand and not react in a negative way. If she did, then what would he do? He had not thought beyond that.

Daisy reached out to him and pulled him back onto her bed. He kissed her gently but pulled back from her and sat up straight, he just needed to get this confession out of the way.

He opened his mouth to tell her, to try and tell her but she was not listening, kissing him and inviting him back to bed. How could he resist? She was beautiful and warm and soft and as he touched her she responded with more passion. As if he had a magic switch, and she just came alive under his fingers. Neither had ever felt such a flow of love and it was so easy, so right. They exhausted each other again and again. He lay beside her and held her in his arms, kissing the top of her head like you would kiss a child. Her hair always had the smell of fresh flowers and he loved that about her. How would she react when he told her? He was terrified she would throw him out and tell her father what had happened. Could he trust her, this woman who was now his reason for living, please God let it not be a dream. She broke the silence and it surprised him because up to now she had asked him very little since that first time they met. Just accepted him as he was, no future, no past, just this, the present, the passion and the love that was growing between them.

"Dom, I think it is time you told me why you are here with Devlin Marshall? She waited. This was it, the moment he had been dreading for so many weeks.

Dom took a deep breath, having rehearsed this moment in his head so many times, but his brain emptied, all he could focus on was her lying there; he kissed her ferociously, tearing at her as if she was tissue paper on a gift, and made love to her once more as if she was the last woman on earth. As if it might be the last time.

There was somebody knocking on the door. Dominic and Daisy froze, jumped out of bed and both ran to the window.   A familiar figure was hammering on the door downstairs.

"It's my Dad," said Daisy with some annoyance in her voice. "What does he want I wonder?"

"Daisy, leave us alone, I need to speak to Dominic," it was an order and not a request. She rarely heard Alex speak to her in this way.

"No, second thoughts, you are coming with me, get dressed, NOW," he directed his request towards Dominic, his anger was rising, just seeing the pair of them half dressed, he ordered Dom to be quick and he almost dragged him out of the apartment.

"What's going on Dad? TELL me," she was mortified at his sudden appearance and his tone.

"Leave it Daisy, I need some answers, and this isn't the moment to explain," Alex spoke to her as he brushed past, almost knocking her over.

He ordered Dom into the passenger seat of his car, Daisy followed them and stood by his car almost in defiance, demanding to know what was going on.

"WHAT answers? Where are you going?" she demanded, but Alex drove away without saying another word.

They drove away, tyres screeching, her father ignoring her pleas, what on earth was going on and why would he do that?

They pulled into a car park on a deserted industrial estate near Newport, and Alex got out of the car and opened the passenger door, ordering Dom to get out.

"Right, I want some answers. Why are you still here?" he was being direct, he had a hundred questions, but this was a start. His tone was less than polite, and Dom was scared. He had been seeing Daisy for a while now and Alex knew about them, so why now? Why the inquisition? Was he worried for his daughter? Understandable for any father, but was there more to this? A hundred questions running through Dom's head.

Dom said nothing for a moment, trying to gather his thoughts and evaluate what to tell this man. If he said too much he was in trouble, it he said too little who knows what he might do. He was acting like an irrational angry man, his eyes were wild with fury.

"Rebecca ," one word from Alex and Dom almost fell to his knees. How the hell did he know about Ria . His brain was racing, his heart pounding even faster than his brain. He opened his mouth to speak but Alex came back with another shock.

"What do you know about Rebecca ? Tell me the truth or I

will kill you," and he meant it. He was madder than he had ever been in his whole life. He pushed Dom over the bonnet of the car and grabbed him by the throat, closing his strong fingers around his throat. This man who he was sure had an involvement with his colleague was now sleeping with his daughter. He could quite easily kill him right there and then just for that.

'Ria ? Ria who?" he sounded pathetic, and Alex swung a punch at him, smashing his fist into his face. Blood was everywhere and Dom howled.

"Again, I give you one more chance… Rebecca, what is your involvement with Ria ? He dragged him upright and swung at him again and hit him full in the stomach. Dom doubled over in pain and Alex kicked him, knocking him over and he splayed onto the gravel, holding up his arm to say no more, no more.

"Ok, Ok, I knew a Ria , it was an accident. I didn't mean to kill her. I didn't see her. She went overboard and Devlin wouldn't go back for her," he was begging for his life here. But he was glad to get it said to somebody, even him. He knew it would be all over with Daisy, that she would not entertain staying with a killer and he would go to jail. He looked defeated and weak lying there in a bloodied heap.

"Get up," Alex was shouting at him. "Get up you snivelling, little sh*t, stay away from my daughter, do you hear me? Stay away…"

Dominic did not reply, he got up and stared at Alex in defiance.

Thinking that Alex would take him back to Cowes, Dom started to walk towards the car, but Alex jumped into the driving seat, locked the doors and drove off. Leaving him standing there. He was done with Dominic Montpelier, and he was going to tell Daisy she was done with him too. It had to end. There was no way he wanted a man like that, with such a dangerous nature to be associated with any daughter of his. To leave that girl and not say anything was reprehensible. The worst kind of crime, hit and run but on a grander scale.

Alex got back to the apartment in Cowes in 20 minutes, and once more hammered on the door but Daisy did not answer, she was gone. She took a call from Dom and went to find her father who didn't wait around in Cowes and drove at breakneck speed back to the Old Mill House.

Daisy was back at the Old Mill House waiting for her father to return. She was livid. Dom had found a phone box and called her at the apartment, he just said "Goodbye Daisy, I am sorry."

"Dom, talk to me what has happened? You sound terrible...TELL me, please," she was desperate in her tone as she quizzed him."

"Please tell me my father hasn't hurt you? Please Dom, did he hit you? What has happened?"

"Something happened on my way to England Daisy, I should have told you, but I was terrified of what you would think. Your father knows about it, I don't know how he knows but he wasn't happy with me, he left me here in the middle of nowhere. I am a real mess Daisy, I didn't recognise him, he was like a man possessed ... I just don't understand why he did that, I'm lucky to be alive! I'm going to walk back to The Copse and try and ring my parents, I need help Daisy, but I don't think we should see each other, I am not worth it. In another life, under different circumstances I think there could be a you and I, but not now. Goodbye Daisy," and he was gone.

She felt sick. There was pain in his voice, she could hear it, he could barely speak. But that was it! No clues, no reason, what the hell had her father done? She wanted answers.

Dom found his way back to The Copse on foot and cleaned himself up but the damage to his face was obvious, Devlin reacted straight away when he saw him at dinner.

"What the hell happened to you?" he grabbed him and inspected his face. "Who did this to you?" he needed to know, so he asked him again.

"Who did this Dom? And why? Where have you been?" Three questions. Dom slumped onto a chair and leaned on the table with his head in his hands; never since he was a child had he wanted to cry so much, but he held it in and just said nothing. Devlin dragged him out of the room, pulling over the chair in the process making a clattering noise that echoed around the huge room. Jamal and his son just looked at each other. He knew this was not good and something not to be shared with the Lesçon's right now. Out in the garden Dom admitted he had spoken to Alex McFarlane, and it had got heated.

"Daisy's father, he knows about Ria , he knows," he could not imagine what Devlin would do or say.

"Did you TELL him? How does he know? How? Just how?" His brain was working overtime, he could not get past how he would find out. Dom must have told him.

"You idiot, did you tell Daisy? Did you tell him? I can't believe it Dom you are in some serious trouble here. We have to get you out of here," Devlin was not waiting for answers, but he stopped and realised he needed to know.

"Tell me, TELL ME" he forced himself to wait for an answer.

"I was with Daisy, and he took me from her apartment, he dragged me out to his car and attacked me, he knew about Ria , he asked me about Ria , I said nothing. He knew, I said it was an accident, then he drove off and left me, I walked back here," he was rambling and sounded confused and scared.

Devlin was thinking and pacing up and down trying to piece it together in his head.

"If he knows they must have found her. They must have somebody who knew you were with her. She is dead so she couldn't have told them anything, why did you say it was an accident? I thought you said nothing."

"He kept saying what do I know about Ria , what was your involvement with Ria ? I just said it was an accident we couldn't save her it was too late."

"My God Dom, you said it was an accident, so he will know you are involved."

Devlin was still pacing up and down and even he was starting to panic, but he had a thought.

"He didn't arrest you, despite the fact he is some kind of policeman. If she was dead he would have arrested you right? Why did he let you go? No evidence obviously. Do they have her, have they found her? I need to find out. You say nothing else do you hear me? NOTHING," Devlin was shouting at him. "You keep away from Daisy, you keep away from all of them next door, do you hear me?"

Dom just nodded, he was devastated. He was just starting to have feelings for Daisy and now that was ruined. What could he do? He needed his family, he would throw himself on their mercy and hope they would help him. It was clear Devlin was not going to and this situation here was getting worse for him and surely, going to get pretty hair-raising from what he could gather from the people that were coming and going, Russians, French men with scars and tattoos, he caught the odd word about goods and boats and money and that awful Maria who could cut you in half with one look.

It didn't sound like legitimate business to him. He needed to get out and soon. He knew about good business, he had been around it all his life, his family had business that made them wealthy and none of it resembled whatever was happening here in this house.

He felt he had woken up but was still in a bad dream and in danger here. He would try and speak to Daisy tomorrow. Leaving her like this was not what he wanted. He needed her help, and she did say she would help him.

Chapter 14

Maria was surprised when Devlin suggested that they took a trip on his boat. Boat? When did he get a boat? In fact she had no idea that he even had access to a boat, he was full of surprises. Yet another question she needed to ask him. She had not even considered how he had got into the country when he first came to see her, after this revelation she was beginning to think he was a resourceful dark horse. Until this moment it hadn't entered her head that he was probably on a wanted list by police and border officials who would probably arrest him on sight so maybe he had no choice but to travel here by boat. She knew very little of his past and just assumed he had lived under the radar for the last ten years.

"Be ready at ten, we are going out and wear flat shoes," He might just as well have slapped her in the face.

"Flat shoes? Flat shoes?" she said it twice in case she had misheard him.

"Flat shoes, we are going on a boat trip," Devlin smiled as he gave the invitation that sounded like an order. Maria was too weary to argue after the glass balcony bedroom argument that she lost, and in any case she was damned curious to find out about this boat. Any clue to his wealth intrigued her, he still dressed well and gave the air of having money but without seeing his bank account she would never really know. The curiosity came from not knowing just how much he got away with ten years ago but even then he would have spent it by now. The next day dawned to a stormy day but he wasn't going to let that stop them. He had decided to sail around the island and moor the boat in Chale Bay so they could talk about what happened ten years ago, an opportunity to discuss this next Operation on their own with the Russian or Jamal and Theo listening. He doubted she had even been to Chale Bay at all. Being in the Bay would be the ideal way to break the ice and get her talking. She had been quiet since the first day back and not made any waves in any of the meetings, just listened and chipped in occasionally. It was not the Maria he remembered and hoped she was in there somewhere. She obviously needed time to re-adjust to her new life after being institutionalised for ten years.

They left Bembridge under a black sky and the threat of a storm as they sailed around the east of the island, around Culver Cliff and Sandown, around Luccombe, Shanklin, Ventnor and into Chale Bay, the sun came out as they arrived within sight of Chale beach, and Devlin shut off the engine and got out a bottle of wine and two glasses. Perfect timing all round. She wanted to know about the boat.

"How long have you had this little beauty? Suits you," she was impressed. She loved nice things but was curious about money and whether he got enough from the heist to pay for it. He had to be careful how he worded his reply, he was not going to tell her the truth.

"I have had it a while but thinking of selling it. Not much use for it if I am going to stay on the island, and I would like to. I love the old place," he laughed as he said it.

He had packed a box of food which surprised Maria; it had been a long time since anybody did anything like that for her. She wasn't sure how to take it. Was it supposed to be a special meal or was he hungry?

They chatted easily as the boat rocked gently on the breeze and drank the bottle of wine; she asked him more questions than he expected. Where had he been for ten years? How did he get away from the beach that night ten years ago, without being caught? And the crunch question…

"How much did you take from the stash of drugs that night?" she went for the jugular, and it took him by surprise. He laughed and opened a second bottle, filling up both glasses again, he was not going to answer that one, instead he said,

"How much do you think I took that night? Did I take anything?" nothing like a question to answer a question to defer an answer.

Now let me ask you something Maria, "How much did you take from Matt before he died?" he waited but she was so shocked she put her glass down and stood up. She lit a cigarette and walked away from him, turning around eventually and looked at him.

"How much do you think I took? Did I take anything?" she smiled because she was pleased with her clever reply, but he was not going to give up. Only he could get away with speaking to Maria Hayward like this, he sensed that she liked his directness.

"I think you took it all, I think you outsmarted him which is why he tried to take his revenge on you, tell me I am wrong, tell me the truth Maria we have to make this work and we need some honesty here. If I can't trust you then this is not going anywhere," he waited again for her answer then continued.

"If this Russian does what he is supposed to do and comes back with positive outcomes then this will be bigger than anything you and Matt did, we are not Maria and Matt, we are Devlin, Maria, Jamal and the Russian, bigger stakes Maria. You and I need to be rock solid to deal with them or they will make mincemeat out of both of us. We are playing with the big boys now right on our own doorstep, no time for games and lies."

"Well that told me," Maria was laughing almost hysterically, and then surprisingly she started to cry, to sob as if her whole world had come crashing down. She didn't stop and he got up and comforted her, holding her tight and very close to him until she stopped shaking and calmed down.

He kissed her on the top of her head, she was grateful for his concern but pushed him away and rubbed her eyes.

"Sorry about that, it has all felt too much to deal with," she admitted. "I seem to have acquired built in waterworks since I got out! I'm ok now, thank you," she took his handkerchief and wiped her eyes.

"Don't mistake that for me being weak will you?" she laughed.

"Never!" he replied quickly.

"Look, I have an idea, and you can tell me to f*...k off if you like but you and I should get married," she looked him straight in the eye as she said it. He sat back in the chair in shock, his brain working overtime trying to absorb her last sentence. One word did come into his thoughts...Jackpot!

"Married?" he nearly choked on his wine but covered his mouth with his hand in an effort to cover his reaction to her suggestion.

"It worked for me and Matt, pretending to be married, got us respect and trust all those years, especially with the Cartels. They seem to like the family, married thing, it was a sham but nothing stopping us making it seem real for all to see," she took a deep breath and hoped he would see her proposal as real and viable. He wasn't going to tell her he had no interest in her, but the same thought had occurred to him. He was actually secretly delighted she had said it. Did she think he did? Just because he packed a box of food and was being kind to her? He didn't speak for a while, he needed to word this properly and she had just revealed something to him that he had wondered about for years. She and Matt were not married! Well that was a revelation. He had no idea. Sensing his reluctance she filled the silence with words that he didn't really hear but could see her lips moving. Was she saying we could take it slow? Dear God, he had thought about getting close to her, but this was maybe one step too far, but there is the house…and the missing money, was this the answer to his prayers? Could he be that mercenary? Well of course he could.

"Ok," he actually said the word but followed it up with, "You and Matt were not married? Seriously? Not actually married? I am shocked to hear that, the whole world thought you two were rock solid, including being married, I don't know what to say, why me? And why not him? We don't know each other really, we have history, but would it work?" A long speech but there was a weak sound of hope in his voice, she had made the suggestion. He felt there was some desperation in her idea. It was no love match, it was no match at all but would be a great act of convenience, for him anyway. Why would she want this? He knew why he would want this but not her. He could only think in the moment that she needed somebody to look after her, to use him maybe as she had obviously used Matt until he was no use then she pounced and killed him. Like a Praying Mantis, he shuddered at the image in his head. Was he prepared to risk that? He had just witnessed a vulnerable Maria, one that the world never saw. He could work with that one, but he would have to watch his back for the ruthless side of Maria.

'Could we keep it quiet for a while until we have worked out how it will work?' was what Devlin wanted to say, but she beat him to it and for that he was extraordinarily grateful in that moment of awkwardness...

"Erm maybe we should keep it to ourselves for a while until we get our heads around it? Maybe just go and do it without any fuss?" She had made up her mind how she wanted to do it. Not wanting to make herself look stupid again over a man who was probably not really interested in her. He would do for now. He was correct in thinking she was going to use him for her own reasons.

Chapter 15

Daisy was furious with her father and slammed through the house like a raging elephant looking for her lost baby.

"Where IS he?" she demanded of Jess.

"What on earth is the matter?" It was a genuine question of concern from Jess, watching her step-daughter rampage through the house, opening and closing doors, looking for Alex. He had not been there since this morning and Jess told her that.

"He has beaten up Dominic and left him out in the lanes on his own, in God knows what state!" She was beside herself with anger.

"What do you mean? Your father wouldn't do that," Jess was firm in her reply.

"Then you don't know him at ALL," she screamed back at Jess.

Chapter 16

It was baking hot in Albuquerque, New Mexico. The Russian mopped his head for the fifth time since landing at the second or was it the third airport in the USA? He was already exhausted from sweating like a pig; his words, describing his dripping state, to a chatty girl in the kiosk at the airport when he ordered a cold drink and a sandwich. After opening it he decided he would rather be hungry, it was unrecognisable and salty. Dire and disgusting.

Luckily for Nikolai Markarov the Cartels were trying to make inroads into Europe with their drug trafficking and there was quite a battle going on between two major gangs in this area alone for supremacy in Europe.

Border control in Europe was the best in the world and they were fighting a constant battle, losing goods to the authorities all the time so they were really going all out to take on a massive drugs drop this year. This was the one they felt had the greatest chance of success. They had tried flying it over, they had tried pleasure cruisers and individuals used as mules. None of them could have the impact of a packed oil tanker, hidden in empty compartments and landed on shore. They liked this idea.

They knew about the failed heist in 1969, it happened all the time, but it was nothing to do with organisation or planning, it came down to one person speaking up and blowing it all to the authorities. They had done their homework. When they find that person who betrayed so many, he or she is dead. Cartel bosses never forget any act of betrayal. If it fails you try again, 'winning' that was their motto, and this time it would succeed.

They had strict instructions to go against all their instincts to treat foreigners with contempt and treat this one with respect.

Nikolai made his way to a roadside motel waiting by the Highway for an unknown vehicle to stop and take him to his contacts, they had his description, and he was certainly distinctive. Eventually he was picked up in a truck that was not luxurious but had air conditioning which meant he could breath for the first time in hours. For that he was grateful. The driver spoke some English and they communicated in broken English and hand signals, he was chewing tobacco and spitting at regular intervals for which he was not grateful. At least he opened the window to do it…small mercies. The dust and the heat blasted inside the truck whenever the window lowered he coughed it up, choked and got rid of the disgusting mess, so Nikolai made the decision not to look, he closed his eyes.

There was nothing really to look at, the landscape was baron, with miles and miles of dry rocky nothing stretching out on all sides. Through the wing mirror of the truck he could see a huge orange dust cloud following them. From a distance it gave the illusion they were being followed by a pack of crazy red dogs. There was a deceptive low lying foggy heat haze, just an illusion that they could not catch up with, stretching out in front of them on the road ahead. The odd vulture flew overhead which was unnerving and the relentless heat pressed down on everything.

He had dealt with these people before, in his former life in Moscow, he came to a similar place with a team of people but this time he was the only one negotiating with this family of Garinos', headed by three brothers who had nine months between them all, like triplets, it was very difficult to tell them apart. A notorious family that you didn't cross or upset. He saw them once, from a distance, and knew them by reputation from some dealings in the past and intended to do neither cross or upset them; if he was lucky he would get out alive with a good deal, if he was not then he would be history. If they didn't like you that was it, end of story.

The truck stopped and the driver asked him to get out in such a tone he would not dare argue, it sounded like an order, and did as bid without complaining, but who could tell in this damned heat. They were not there yet, they were surrounded by desert on all sides, no houses to be seen and he had no idea where he was. The two in the back of the truck jumped out and blindfolded him then told him to get back into the truck. He never understood this ritual, how would he know where he was in this vast faceless landscape that spread over hundreds of miles and looked the same mile after mile. His heart was beating fast, but he expected this as the norm in this situation. He had no idea how long they were on the road, but it was minutes and not hours for which, once again he was truly grateful in this killer heat.

The truck stopped and he was ordered out, the driver shouting to him to take off the blindfold and as he adjusted his eyes in the relentless, blinding sun he caught the back end of the driver as he disappeared into one of the small shacks around the square.

He looked down surprised to see at his feet a variety of small children and many more chickens than children all standing, quite still, in what looked like red dust in the square quadrangle arrangement of tiny red single storey houses with matching red doors. It amused him, as if they had a consignment of red paint and needed to use it all up. They were all staring at him. They had never seen a man so tall or one with such strange black and white hair. They had driven through huge wooden doors attached to a tall red rough block brick wall, he estimated must be 20 feet tall and surrounded the square he was standing in. The giant doors were now being closed and locked making this like a mini-fortress, one way in and the same way out.

He was led into a surprisingly large kitchen and made to feel very welcome by an old lady with very few teeth and a weather beaten face, her wrinkles were like a road map in a busy town. She gave him a beer and he thanked her, then kissed her hand. He had no idea why he did that, maybe to ingratiate himself to at least one of them, it seemed to do the trick, she smiled a toothless grin and gave him a second bottle of beer, after flicking numerous flies off the table with a white cloth she had in her hand, she put it in front of him. She led him to a room just off the kitchen with gestures rather than speech, he gathered her English wasn't that good. The room was clean and adequate, no more. He dropped his bag on the small bed and held his head under the tap which felt so good after the dust and heat of the journey. He was to be there for a week, that was the plan. They were good hosts and more and more men who all looked similar were brought in to meet him and they had endless meetings, sometimes he wasn't sure if it was a meeting or a social event, they all seemed to drift into the same thing, one beer after another, lots of back slapping and table thumping and poring over maps in hot, dusty rooms with low ceilings that made life feel claustrophobic. He was very careful about how much alcohol he consumed so he didn't let his guard down. He gave the illusion of being a drinker but not much actually went down his throat. A trick he learned many years ago in situations such as this, the company of dangerous men with guns in their belts meant, if you wanted to survive, you kept your wits about you. He trusted no-one and felt trouble was only the thickness of a red wall away. He slept light and locked his door at night when each days' discussions were over. The highlight of most discussions were the maps he had brought with him, they were fascinated by the Isle of Wight nestled at the foot of England and asked many questions. Some could not believe the island was only twenty two miles across by eleven miles and had its own airport and many beaches and marinas. He explained the intricacies of deserted beaches at the bottom end of the island and how there was 57 miles of shoreline to drop goods that were open and lacking any kind of rigorous coastguard scrutiny, and anyway they had men in those offices paid to turn a blind eye when it was necessary, he went through their plans for receiving the goods into England and the distribution network. They were particularly impressed with its geographical closeness to Europe and France and many nodding heads agreed this was a good way to get their goods into Europe.

He had taken photographs with him of the island, and these where the highlight of the first meeting, they went down well, not believing how green it was. A stark contrast to their own landscape.

The tankers were arranged, the same Company as before. The drugs would be flown to one of them for the pick-up at Freeport, just south of the Gulf of Mexico, and on to England. Nikolai had many contacts in Russia for small arms and ammunition, it only took a phone call, and it would all be arranged, but it would be different this time, no arms from the USA, all coming in on a separate tanker from the same Company but from South Africa. The network was already set up, just a location and a time needed. They favoured the first week in September, the 1st and 2nd, Saturday and Sunday, he said yes to that. The crew in England would be ready, they would have to be.

They were used to these consignments going all over the world but not yet Europe, so they were as excited by the plans as he was to agree to take the drugs. It was going smoothly, too smoothly.

More of the family had appeared and he was grateful that most of them spoke English with bits of Spanish here and there, he understood Spanish well enough. They were impressed that he could speak the language and the planning that had already gone into this.

Nikolai came with good references from Jamal Lesçon who was an old friend of the Garinos brothers, but he was not Jamal, and they would have been happier to see him here. Trust was the big one. Like stepping off a cliff and trusting there was a net ten foot down to catch you even when you can't see it, but you have been told it is there. That flimsy.

Day 6 seemed hotter than ever, it was unbearable, Nikolai didn't really sleep and dragged himself up out of bed just after dawn, bathed in sweat. He was thinking about ending this trip and getting out of here. Nothing more to be discussed, he couldn't do any more. He hoped they were happy but who would know. Today he needed them to drop him back at the motel so he could reverse his nightmare journey back to England. The lure of cool air back in England, was almost overwhelming, his impatience was crushing him, but each time he thought it was done they brought in someone else to shake his hand and it started all over again, the beer, the table slamming, the maps. He wandered into the kitchen to find a drink and some air, opening the stable door of the kitchen he was met with a breeze of sorts, it was warm air but moving air, which was rare, and welcome at that moment. He closed his eyes and let the air hit his face.

He sat on a small wall outside and looked around him. The red buildings, all joined together were fascinating and he wondered about the occupants, did they live their whole lives in this isolation and damned heat? Was it this nightmare environment driving them on with this drugs business to get out of here no matter what how illegal? The idea of wealth and freedom, part of him could understand it. Knowing what it was like to be hunted. Money was freedom, he would make this work. This was no way to live with this stifling environment and oppressive heat. How did they function? There was no sign of life yet, it was very early. He had lost track of time but thought it was about 5 a.m.. Something caught his eye as he sat contemplating this place, what he was doing, and his desire to be out of it. The huge wooden doors moved. He screwed up his eyes and focussed again, yes they were open, only slightly but they were not locked, and the breeze was moving them slowly. He sat staring at the doors for a few minutes then went back inside. What was happening here? He had seen the ritual of door closing too many times this week to know that was unusual. Should he alert them? Were they in danger here? Why were those doors open? His head was whizzing with options, he had to think quick.

Inside the kitchen he was met with another surprise. On the table was a pile of money, a huge pile of money and a set of keys. He stopped dead in his tracks staring at the table. For a second his instincts told him to grab and run.

Run for your life, get out of there, they are giving you the chance to go. The gates are open, the keys to the truck are within your grasp and money for your trouble. Somebody had put this here while he was outside! He had just passed this table and there was nothing on it ten minutes ago.

It had all gone well, but was he deluding himself? Part of him thought they didn't trust him, did he trust them? Was there trust on both sides? As he looked around he spotted a photograph in a silver frame on the dresser. It was a family, parents, kids, grandparents and he thought of his own family, it bought him back down to earth with a bump. His wonderful wife in hiding in Paris with his children who needed their father in their lives. He never needed them more than at this moment, but their future depended on his success here and he was not going to fail and be shot as he ran, as wretched as it all was and felt.

Don't risk this, it's a test. That's it a test. They are testing me. He turned his back on the table and went to the sink, filled his cup with water, drank it and placed the cup next to the pile of money and keys on the table and sat down and shouted. "Hello, is anybody awake," he hit the metal cup over and over with a metal spoon making enough noise to wake the whole house.

One of the men involved in the talks this week… Pedro, the grandson of the old lady, came too quickly for him to have been asleep, he was dressed with his gun in his hand.

"What's happening?" Pedro stopped dead in his tracks when he saw Nikolai sitting at the table banging a metal cup with a spoon, thinking the mad tall man with the crazy hair had gone even crazier. In Spanish he uttered something that sounded like 'Persona estúpida' not difficult to translate! He was right, it was a test. He told the boy the gates were open, and he pushed the keys towards the boy with the spoon. Nikolai watched him from the doorway run towards the doors and lock them, stirring up a massive red cloud of dust than engulfed him as he ran.

It occurred to him as he watched the red cloud that he had not met the Garinos brothers on this trip. Would they appear now or was he to be spared that after the test? He hoped the latter, they instilled fear and mayhem wherever they went. They obviously didn't live here, and why would they want to. Money had freed them from the red walls. He wanted to be free and hoped that today would be the day.

His gut feeling about meeting the brothers manifested itself that afternoon.

The gates were opened, and men stood in line at either side, waiting… ten minutes later, three, sleek black, bullet proof limo's arrived in a blare of horns and cheers. They got out of the cars and fired their guns in the air in defiance. Defiance of what Nikolai had no idea, but their entrance was noisy and pointless as far as he could see. Is that how they ruled here? With fear, of course it was, poor sods he thought.

The brothers summoned Nikolai to the usual meeting room, guns on the table and arms folded. An hour in that room and he was unsure if he had won them over or not, so many questions. The suspicion was clear and had trickled up the pecking order to them, thus their visit. In their wisdom they decided that they needed some kind of sweetener to get this thing going and prove their new English target was serious and not another amateur attempt at moving their goods. Their rivals in El Paso had lost millions dealing with people from England and that was not going to happen to them without some kind of goodwill gesture to prove they were serious.

Nikolai assured them that they meant business now and in the future and offered them exactly what they were looking for. 50 carats of diamonds, delivered to an office in Hatton Garden, to be picked up by their contact in London, today. They left the room, he assumed to consider his offer. Nikolai had been in this position before and was ready. One phone call back to England and the diamonds would be delivered personally, then the deal would be done, and he would be free. He hoped, and for the first time since he left the cool sanctuary of England, he prayed.

The brothers did not return to the meeting room, he heard the cars leave and was left sitting there wondering if he would ever get out of there. The door at the end of the room opened and a small man with a thick black moustache came in and sat opposite Nikolai.

"Make the call," he pushed his chair away and left him sitting there.

They were not stupid these people, the price of diamonds was rocketing to an eye watering level and Nikolai knew that;   he estimated 40,000 dollars a carat right now and rising fast. He was glad to have the back up from his source. They would fetch 2 million on any market, surely it would be enough to seal this trust between them.   He would call him and get this thing going. He forgot it was 3 am in England and the call was not the best clear line.   The diamonds would be taken personally to Hatton garden this morning and be there before noon.   Nikolai thanked him and hung up. Now it was a waiting game.

Chapter 17

Alex and Jess McFarlane were still in love, just as much as the day they met in Cowes, on the seafront back in 1969 when she was trying to find a house to buy on the island. She looked at him now as she did then.

It was still early, they had both woken early and when she realised he was not in bed, got up to find him having breakfast in their cosy kitchen, she stood at the sink watching him in the reflection of the window, remembering her thoughts the first day she met him, she recalled everything from those first few minutes she set eyes on him, the attraction was instant…

He had a beautiful voice, everything about him was beautiful, from his perfect white teeth to his thick black hair that was coiffured within an inch of its life! Jess was transfixed and her brain was going ever so slightly to mush just standing there listening. This was not good. He was wearing a black sweater and light-coloured trousers with a shirt so white she found herself comparing it to the colour of his teeth. Jess was melting where she stood on the pavement, thinking to herself that this should NOT be happening. She was not interested in him, she was NOT…

But she was interested in him within ten minutes of them meeting, and it was mutual, they had loved each other passionately for ten years. Only this morning … after the phone call at 3 a.m. he nuzzled up to her and she was rendered helpless after just one kiss on her neck, she just adored this man, it was as if he was part of her and she was incomplete without him. He made love to her as it if was the first time, they just melted into each other in a soft, warm sexy wave of passion. Like a love scene in a movie it was perfect. She fell asleep and he waited until he was sure she was fast and would not be disturbed as he got out of bed to get ready for his trip later. Opening the safe behind the secret panel he took out 50 diamonds and put them into a black velvet bag. There were plenty more in there and this would seal the deal that would bring more wealth to the family. Wealth that had been stolen away from his family, years ago, but they had not forgotten. Nikolai was family and he was glad to help him get his own family back. He was glad she didn't wake, he would grab some breakfast and be in London in just over two hours delivering the diamonds that would complete Nikolai's deal with the Cartel.

Nikolai, his cousin Nikolai. He owed him big time, he got him back to England all those years ago after he emptied the strong boxes in Zurich, got him back to England risking everything. He knew that one day he would be able to repay him, and this was the time.   Alex, Alexei, his mother Alexandra Markarov and Nikolai's father Peter Markarov were brother and sister. It would have to remain a secret. Jess would never understand such family loyalty. She had no idea he was Russian by birth, no-one did.

Lately though she thought he had been distant and sometimes she heard him having really odd phone calls. He had a haphazard lifestyle but lately even more chaotic. Nothing odd about phone calls but she thought she heard him speaking in another language, she thought Russian. She was not supposed to be there and had come home earlier than planned. He laughed at her as said it must have been the radio she heard but she was convinced… and now another call but this time it was 3 am. Never in ten years had she known him to take calls at that time of day. However strange she had decided she would not ask him again, there had to be trust and his was not a 9 – 5 job.

Jess was thinking about phone calls and Daisy and the anger she showed on her last visit. She was struggling to come to terms with what Alex had done to Dominic and her head was all over the place. Divided loyalties, should she say something to Alex or just leave it be and hope it all went away. Whose side should she take? Alex or Daisy? Maybe Dom was exaggerating, and they had just had an argument. Maybe Daisy was exaggerating, and it wasn't as bad as Dom made out. Her thoughts were interrupted by the phone ringing in the hall, she got up to answer, hoping it was Daisy but as soon as she heard the voice she sat down on a chair with such force it almost toppled over.

"Hello?"

"Is that you Jess?" a voice from the past. Jess froze

"Jess?"

"I know it's a shock, hear me out please, I would like to speak to you, I would like to see you, please," her voice tailed off and Jess still hadn't spoken.

"Jess, talk to me,"

"Maria, I didn't think I would hear from you again, I'm not sure we have anything to say to each other after all this time. We have both moved on," Jess screwed up her face, hoping Maria would put the phone down. But she did not, she kept talking.

"Jess, I have things I need to say to you but not on the phone please, will you meet me somewhere? Tomorrow?"

To give herself time to think of a suitable reply she just delayed her decision.

"Just say where and what time and I will think about it," was the best offer Jess could come up with. It was such a shock to get that phone call out of the blue after ten years. It had been weeks since Maria had returned to The Copse after being released from prison so why choose today to call her?

"Ok, maybe a pub for lunch? One…ish? What about the Hare and Hounds at Arreton? I hope you can make it," and she put the phone down, not waiting for a reply.

Jess was shocked to hear from Maria after so long and the thought of meeting her made her feel sick. She just kept going over and over the dreadful night that Matt was killed by Maria. Did she really want to be seen out with a convicted murderer? The island was a small place and people would remember. She wished they had picked a bench on the seafront, it would have been less public than a busy pub at lunch time.

What should she do? What would Alex suggest? Should she tell him? Decisions, decisions. Alex was away, he had gone up to London, so she couldn't ask him, he suddenly announced he had to leave straight away after breakfast and wouldn't be back for a few days. He didn't tell her the real reason; he was heading to Hatton Garden then booking himself into a hotel to wait for Nikolai's return. Daisy had gone back to Cowes in a rage over her father's treatment of Dominic so talking to her would be a waste of time.

The next day she felt differently, what could Maria possible have to say to her? Curiosity won the argument going on in her head, 'to go or not to go?' so she got herself ready and drove through Arreton to the Hare and Hounds. It was in the middle of the countryside, a thatched pub with so much character; a place she went often with Alex and Daisy. There were lots of nooks and crannies inside the building, booths and places tucked away in alcoves, with old fireplaces and a great atmosphere. She found Maria sitting at a table away from the main hub of the restaurant and Jess was pleased. There was no hugging or immediate joy to see each other, and it felt awkward, but Jess had thought of several questions as she drove towards the pub and was curious to find out what Maria wanted. Why had she summoned her here? They were good friends for many years, Jess was one of few people that Maria had time for.

She had already ordered a bottle of wine and two glasses so that was out of the way, alleviating the necessity for endless conversation about sweet or dry, white or red. Jess didn't want to eat, it felt wrong somehow to sit opposite someone who had done what she had done and eat food. The atmosphere was strange from both women, Maria didn't have any expectations and was surprised that she turned up at all.

"What do you want Maria?" her tone was frosty. She didn't know how else to be under the circumstances. Pleasantries and compliments did not seem appropriate, in the past they would have been nice to each other.

"Before I say anything I want to tell you how sorry I am for what happened. I know what I did was too awful for words, and if I could think about it and go back I would never have done what I did," she waited with her head down. She was finding it difficult to look at Jess but continued. "I was in shock after what Matt tried to do to me and I reacted instead of getting help…"

"Could we not talk about all that please," Jess was firm and determined not to discuss it anymore.

"Ok I understand, but I do have things I want to ask you Jess and I may have things to tell you," she was being very cagey, and Jess was intrigued.

"I hear that you and Alex are still together, I have to say I am surprised," it was a statement and not a question.

"We got married, ten years now, and why wouldn't we be together?"

"Married! Well my dear, what I have to tell you might come as a shock to you, and I am not sure how much Matt told you about our business?" she looked at Jess waiting for an answer.

"Not much, well nothing actually, not a thing except he was never in one place for more than five minutes!" Jess recalled.

"There are things that he left unresolved when he died, things I have never been able to, how shall I put this? Unscramble I think describes it nicely," she took a large swig of her wine and continued. Jess looked at her watch feeling impatient and wanting this to end.

"The money side of things of our business I am talking about. I have had years to sit and think and try and work things out and I have come to the conclusion that your Alex knows more than he lets on, I think he has secrets. I would bet my new house you don't know about them," she laughed.

"Why are you laughing? Are you laughing at me or my husband. Don't you dare laugh at us," Jess was fuming and stood up to leave.

"Sit down, I am not laughing at you or him.

"I don't have much to laugh at these days. Just the thought

of me betting on anything, is funny, I don't know what is real and what is fantasy these days. My house is full of men I don't really like, my house isn't really my house, they have taken over, French, Russian… Nothing is as it was. But I didn't ask you to come to hear about me Jess. I want to ask you about you," she looked at Jess as she spoke, and Jess looked at her for the first time.

"Well I will give you that, the house certainly has changed, I love it actually, Devlin gave me the grand tour before you came back," she admitted.

"Did he now? I heard he came to your place for drinks," Maria was curious now.

"Yes, I walked up there one day and was surprised to see him inside the house, and he invited me in; I only met him once, but he remembered me. They have done a brilliant job, I love all the glass and especially the room with the glass balcony, very impressive," she trailed off and stopped talking. Maria was listening intently, it occurred to Jess that most definitely it was not like her at all to let anybody finish a sentence.

"He came to see me in prison, and it seemed like a good idea to get him to move in for a while, keep an eye on the place, I quite like having him around, but then I always did," she said thoughtfully. "I've missed you Jess," she waited for a reply to that statement, Jess wasn't sure what to say.

"Well we go a long way back, must say I thought about

coming to see you, but wasn't sure you would want that so I kept away," she was careful in her reply, not actually saying the words 'I missed you too,' which would have been a half truth.

Things she wanted to say to Jess she was now having second thoughts about, so she hesitated. Perhaps Jess was not ready for this revelation. Maybe not tell her today. This didn't seem the moment to load this meeting with too much information.

"I didn't see anybody, just my Solicitor and the last few months Devlin turned up, he tried over the years, but it is no place to see anybody," she then surprised Jess by saying she had to go.

"Jess I have to go, let's do this again sometime when I have got my head together a bit more. Devlin and I have plans so my head is full right now, trying to adjust etc.. please can we do this again? I meant it when I said I missed you," and with that she got up, threw money on the table to pay the bill and left. Jess sat there and watched her through the small window drive off in her MG.

"That was a waste of time," she told Alex when he returned two days later. "She said she wanted to see me and had things to tell me then, apart from saying sorry – nothing," she was indignant at wasting a lunchtime on an indifferent meeting.

"I expect she finds it hard after ten years inside trying to hold normal conversations, she must be institutionalised in some way. Are you going to keep in touch? How do you feel about her now?" Alex asked with some curiosity. The thought of his wife and a convicted murderer wasn't one he savoured but understood they had been friends for a long time.

"She said she wished she could go back and undo it all and she was sorry for what she did, so I suppose that's something, guess what… she missed me!" Jess was wistful and wandered off to another part of the house, leaving Alex in the kitchen.

The phone rang and Jess ran back into the kitchen waving her hands in the air as if to say, you get it, I'm not here, just in case it was Maria again.

She heard Alex say, "just hang on a sec I'll get her for you."

"It's her again, go on, find out what she wants." Reluctantly and with a lot more hand waving Jess picked up the receiver.

"Hello."

"Jess, I'm sorry, I didn't say all the things I wanted to say to you. Meet me on Friday, same place, same time. I need to tell you stuff," and then after a few seconds of silence she added, "I would like you to do something for me next Wednesday if you are free, 11 a.m.," she didn't wait for Jess to reply, and the phone went dead. Jess looked at the phone and said out loud, 'why do you do that Maria? End conversations with a question and not wait for an answer.'

Friday came and Jess was in two minds whether to go and meet her again. What could she possibly want her to do next Wednesday?

"Curiosity will take you there," Alex was laughing and looking quizzical at the same time. He could not think of anything he would allow Jess to do for Maria, not that his permission would be needed. Jess was her own woman and did what she wanted, they had no secrets. Well she had none from him. He kept things from her, thinking she did not need to know; was that the same thing as keeping a secret? From his point of view no, he was protecting her from dangerous people.

Chapter 18

"Definitely NO, sorry Maria it would be so wrong to do that. I just couldn't. I can't even put into words why I can't but please ask somebody else.

"But I don't have anybody else Jess. I never really did. You have always been my only real friend. Please Jess, at least think about it," Maria was pleading with her.

"Is this why you asked me to come here today? You could have asked me last time or on the phone," she started gathering up her scarf and keys and bag.

"Jess don't go, I have other things to say to you and it's important. I am going to marry Devlin with or without you being my friend and my witness, but if you can't then you can't. I can move on from that. In time I hope we can be friends again. I need a friend right now. Devlin is good to me, and I think he cares for me, maybe he might even come to love me, but don't hold your breath with that one!" she laughed as she said it.

"Then why are you marrying him?" Jess had to ask.

"It's a very good question Jess and there are things in my life that you don't need to know about. I need somebody strong by my side to look after me. He has the best deal, if he marries me he will be secure… with the house and everything. So I can see why he would agree to it. I should have married Matt, it was too late in the end, but it might have made things better between us. We drifted apart in so many ways. A woman needs a man beside her, it is 1979 you know," and she laughed again. A nervous, insecure little laugh.

"I know what you mean, I don't know what I would do without Alex, he is such a rock. I know you never got to know him, but he is so strong, and I am lucky to have him," that was all Jess was going to tell Maria about herself and her life. Just small talk. She was thinking just get on with it Maria, tell me what you have to tell me.

"I need to ask you about Martin Squire and Devlin, what do you know about them? Do you know anything? Have people been talking over the years?" She waited for Jess to digest the question. Jess was perplexed by the subject. Why on earth would she ask her about them?

"I'm not sure what you mean…I don't think I know anything about them," she replied. This wasn't strictly true, as Alex had told her Martin Squire and Devlin were both wanted by Interpol for some major jewel thefts in Europe years ago but that wasn't going to leave her lips today.

"Jess I want you to trust me and take this no further. Please if you have any sense you won't share this with Alex," it was a request that surprised Jess.

"We have no secrets, so I am not sure I could keep anything

from him," she replied.

"Look, I am going to tell you something about Alex and it might be connected to Martin Squire and Devlin. I have kept this to myself all these years and only you can have this information. What you do with it is up to you, but I think you won't take it back to Alex," she was being very evasive and the curiosity from Jess was obvious.

"Just tell me Maria, just tell me," Jess was being firm as her patience grew thinner.

"I am sorry to remind you of the night… well you know when Matt…"

"Yes, no need to go over that again," Jess didn't want to hear about it now and the next bit of information shocked her to the core. It was the last thing she expected Maria to tell her, and indeed she probably would not be able to speak to her husband about it, as it was very clearly something he was not telling her.

"After I shot Matt, Alex threw me onto your sofa. I sat there for some time, in shock," she hesitated,

"Yes I know, and I can't imagine how you felt Maria, shock is a terrible thing and I know what you went through up at The Copse was horrific and not something any of us could cope with," she was being very kind for the first time, and it was not lost on Maria who had a very uncharacteristic tear in her eye. She was so grateful that

Jess was at least coming round to being friendly to her. It wasn't much but she was listening, and a tiny spark of empathy had emerged during the last few minutes.

"I have re-lived that moment over and over and over and over, to the point I have nightmares about it. But not for the reasons you think. Yes I had done something terrible and could not take it back. I knew what was coming and apart from feeling half dead from the smoke I was terrified for myself and the police and courts and prison. I knew what was coming," she paused for breath.

Jess let her continue, she knew she was building up to something and had no idea what.

"Did you know Alex took the gun off me and put it up high on a shelf so I couldn't use it again?" She looked straight at Jess to make sure she was fully listening to what she was saying, "I was grateful for that, because I was so angry that day who knows what else I would have done."

"Yes I knew that I was there calling the police, then I took Daisy upstairs out of the way, I remember doing that," Jess was recalling that day when Daisy had a gun in her hand, a gun they had both found weeks before, after two men had broken into the Old Mill House and taken Alex, mistaking him for someone else. Jess hid the gun above the fireplace, hidden behind the beam. Daisy was only 14 and saw Jess hide it.

The night Maria shot Matt, Daisy had come downstairs when she heard the shouting in the kitchen and her father being threatened by Matt; she remembered the gun hidden in the fireplace, took it out and aimed it at Matt, but Maria came into the house, stood beside Daisy and shot Matt in front of them all.   She never really knew who the gun belonged to, and never really questioned it since.

'Well did you know he took the gun off Daisy and hid it?" She was beside herself wanting an answer to that one.

"No I didn't, I wasn't in the room was I?" she replied curtly. "I never really thought about that gun. Yes, now I think about it, what happened to that gun? Why do you ask? I don't understand why it is so important," snapped Jess. What was she trying to say?

"Where did he hide it Jess? And what did he do with it? Has he still got it?" She was pleased with herself for finding a route through this. Jess was transfixed by the questions.

"How would I know? I just told you, I hadn't thought about it until this minute. I didn't ask then and I probably won't ask now. Why is it so important?" she asked again.

"Well, if I am honest the location of the gun is immaterial, but I am going to ask you another question Jess, and my guess is you won't know the answer.   Will you be honest with me? Promise?" Maria sat back on her chair and took a sip of her drink, fishing the cherry out and sucking it off the stick as if in victory.

"What question? I am honest Maria," the irony of that answer was not lost on either of them, knowing she had an affair with Matt for five years and said nothing, but neither women mentioned that even if they were thinking it.

"Do you know the combination of the safe," there she had asked. The only way she could. Asking if Jess knew the house had a safe might have evoked a yes answer just to alleviate any embarrassment that she didn't actually know.

"The safe? What safe?" enquired Jess. Just what Maria expected, she had no idea.

"The safe in your house," a bombshell statement that Maria delivered with some satisfaction. If Jess didn't know then Maria might persuade her to come over to Maria's side on this.

Jess said nothing for a few minutes. What is she talking about. She needed to think quick but was struggling with this one.

"Erm, I think I remember somebody saying there was a safe, but we don't use it," lied Jess thinking Maria would be happy with that response and leave it there.

"You have no idea do you?" Maria waited.

Jess felt defeated. Maria was not playing games here, she was serious. Why she was interested in the safe she had no idea but hearing about it made her feel sick.

"Jess, I can tell by the expression on your face, this is the first you have heard about a safe in your house. Come on, I asked you to be honest with me. We all want our men to be straight with us, up front, honest, no secrets, but I am telling you – there is a safe in your house. A Biiiiiiig safe, and I saw it that night. Alex opened it and put the gun inside. He moved packs of money and a pile of stuffed black velvet bags to one side and shoved the gun inside. It was FULL Jess, full, " she waited for Jess to react or respond. "I haven't mentioned this to another living soul Jess. But I think you need to know."

Jess just sat there, in a state of shock. That feeling you get at school when the teacher catches you doing something against the rules. No point denying it if Maria had seen it. How should she play this? She would die for Alex, take a bullet for him but this was something unbelievable and would never have expected to hear in a million years. Staying as calm as she could more detail was needed here, she had no choice but to ask questions instead of her usual acceptance of situations. There was no way Maria was walking out of here without telling her where this safe is.

"Where is it? The safe, where is it?" she was blunt.

"Hidden behind a panel to the right of your fireplace, so you didn't know," she confirmed, then apologised to Jess for upsetting her.

"Look Jess I am sorry, but it's been playing on my mind, I suspect I might know what is in that safe, or what was in it, but I have no proof, I will show you if you like.   When is Alex out next? It will take me two minutes, it is engrained on my brain. I have a mental picture in my head, and that picture has been there for ten years,"

"I will look for it myself and if I can't find it you can come over. What do I do Maria? Why is he hiding a safe full of whatever it is? What is it full of?"

"Well it was full of money, I saw it," Maria said it again.

"On second thoughts, if I am honest I don't want to look for it myself. Come and show me, tomorrow, Alex won't be there all day, he is back in London again until after the weekend, will you come?" she asked Maria for help. They finished their drinks and left the pub together.

Chapter 19

"Do you Devlin, take this woman…"

Jess watched as the two of them legalised their relationship whatever it was. Not quite believing she was there, but it was the only condition Maria made when agreeing to show Jess where the safe was in The Old Mill House.

It was huge, made of ornate black iron with an ugly plain handle and looked menacing when the panel clicked open. It was locked and no sign of any clue to the combination. Jess looked at it and hated what it stood for, lies and deceit. Something she would never ever have thought to accuse Alex of, but there it was in all its glory. Sitting there the dials and handle even looked like a face, staring at her, it had been hidden all this time. How he must be laughing at her on his smug, secretive, high horse. Her wonderful Alex who was perfect in every way, this man that she adored with her heart and soul. Was she so blinded by love that he used that as a weakness to hide this huge secret? Did he have some kind of secret life? All these thoughts made her feel lost in the ridiculous feelings of Alex having a secret life. No surely not, that is so extreme, a secret life! But he had a secret safe for God's sake…Why?

Why would he not mention it, how had she missed it and what to do about it? Was it worth challenging him about it? The fact dawned on her that Maria was the only person in the world that would understand any conversation about it. How on earth could she approach it with Alex? Her world was crashing around her and that feeling of being overwhelmed, not being able to hang on to the sides to stop herself falling into despair. Marias invitation to go back up to The Copse for a drink felt like a lifeline, her ability to gauge the situation was spot on, knowing Jess would not want to be in the house right now.

Maria explained the house was full of men and said they would stay out of their way if they knew what was good for them, girl time. Jess remembered her saying the house was full of French and Russians when they first met in the Hare and Hounds, it would be interesting to see but not if they were banished!

Jamal, Theo and Devlin were all there, apparently upstairs in the office, so they went into the garden. There was no sign or mention of Dominic who had not been seen since Daisy burst into the house looking for her father, shouting that he had attacked Dom. She had not seen Daisy either since that day and wasn't taking calls in her office or answering the phone at the apartment.

Who was this man she thought she knew so well, attacking Dom, hiding a safe, what else wasn't he telling her? A complete feeling of helplessness washed over Jess, not even vaguely knowing what to do, even being there at The Copse with Maria was better than being in her own home right now. Needing and accepting the company and somebody to talk to about this thing that was thrashing around in her head and was definitely going to help. None of it made sense. The sky was blue and there was a warm breeze, not that Jess noticed, she had other things to think about apart from the weather. Maria was talking to her about what was in the safe. She missed some of it but eventually looked up at her and listened.

"I know it's hard for you Jess but think back, to the time, just after I went away. Did Alex do anything out of the ordinary?" it was an odd question.

"What do you mean? Out of the ordinary? I don't understand," Jess was confused by the question, but Maria continued.

"Look I always liked you Jess, I have said it before, but I am going to say it again. There are not many people I trust or like and you are probably it in actual fact. I had a long list of business acquaintances back then but my friend base then, and even more so now, is zero. I am not looking for sympathy," she laughed an ironic laugh. "It's a fact, I don't mix, I don't join in, I don't make friends. You and I go back a long time and if I was in trouble you would be the only person I would go to. I have done some things in my life that I am not particularly proud of, and of course I include what I did to Matt. Things that needed to be done at the time because I had no choice. Matt and I were mixed up in some pretty hair raising stuff business wise and I will never talk about that, you don't need to know. But that is not my personal life, it is not how I think about you. You are real, the business is abstract. Sorry that doesn't make much sense. The business drives me to be the boss, I have to do

that, it is in me to take over, I am sure you have seen that in me?"
She held both her hands out in front of her as if to say you know
what I mean.

"Well I think I know exactly what you mean," replied Jess.
Maria was a one off and blustered her way through life all those years
ago. Jess never understood what she did in her business life, keeping
it very private, and Jess never asked. Her way or the highway in the
old days. Jess understood her and knew she meant no harm to her.
Maria Hayward was a loner and the thought of her not really having
many friends never crossed Jess's mind. But yes she seemed to be
the one friend and the irony, now, even Jess realised both of them
were lacking in friends. At this moment there was huge relief to have
another woman to talk to that was not Daisy.

"Without telling you too much, Matt and I made money and
a lot of it went missing. I thought Matt had taken it, but it turns out
he didn't. He was convinced I had taken it, which is why he tried to
kill me. It disappeared from boxes in a vault in a bank in Zurich.
Matt went to take it all and the boxes were empty. There now you
know why he did what he did. I have never told another soul about
that, not even at the trial. I need a drink, hang on I'll go and get a
bottle," she left Jess sitting there thinking about the enormity of
what Maria had just divulged and wondering what would come next.
It was a week for revelations for sure. Surely there can't be much
more.

It felt like a giant, complicated jigsaw puzzle and it was mashing her head. Was she trying to say Alex is involved in all of this? Was she kidding herself? Surely not, how could he? How could he possibly be involved? All this was washing around her head waiting for Maria to come back, but a few minutes later, coming back down the stairs Maria was shouting. Her voice was raised, but muffled? Something about my car…

Jess got up and went into the house, walking through the huge glass doors into the living room. Maria was coming down the stairs with the local newspaper in her hands. She was livid and shouting Devlin to come downstairs. Spreading the newspaper on the table, Jess read the front page headline about a car crashing and bursting into flames in Ventnor. Reading further down it said something about eye-witnesses seeing the car, a Daimler was in pursuit of a canary yellow MGB hurtling through Shanklin and Ventnor. Both men inside were killed when their car exploded after rolling down the steep hill.

"MY car! It sounds like MY car. Jamal said Dom took my car. The police found it in Newport with the keys still in it, abandoned, Devlin sent somebody from the garage in the village to go and collect it. I am trying to get my head around this story Jess, what does it mean. This car that crashed and burst into flames killing the two men inside was chasing the MG. Were they chasing Dom, or did they think I was in the car? It has to be MY car they are talking about, Jamal said he saw large Daimler parked in the Lane just before Dom left, were they looking for me? Oh my God Dev, I am scared now," she sounded frantic knowing she might be in danger at some point. This was too close to home.

"Does it say who the people were, those that died in the crash?" Jess asked the obvious question and Maria read out loud from the article in front of her, running her finger down the page as she consumed the article.

"Erm… yellow car drove off, Daimler, unidentified… no, they don't know who they are, that makes it worse, eye-witnesses said it was two men in the Daimler, one in the sports car, who were they?"

"Look don't worry, it was an accident, maybe they put two and two together and made five," Devlin joined in the conversation, he genuinely had no idea about any of it. It made him think about security at that moment and called a meeting for later that day. They needed an armed guard on the house for sure now. If somebody was going after Maria they needed to be ready. The Russian was returning from London in the next couple of days and he would complete their circle with major detail of the planned drop later in the summer, he said 1st and 2nd of September in his short phone call. He had probably stirred up a hornets nest with the Cartels, names would have been mentioned and the Cartel from El Paso might have been alerted. They seemed to know about the movements of every scorpion in the desert when it changed nests.

Jess offered to ask Alex if he knew who the men were who died, they might have asked the Press not to release the names. Maria and

Devlin looked at each other and said no, don't worry it doesn't matter, words to that effect. Jess decided she was going to ask anyway.

The conversation about the safe did not continue. Maria was distracted with the County Press and was reading it over and over as if to get clues.

In Cowes, Dom was reading the same article and the thoughts that occurred to him at the time reared their heads again.

"I don't think they were after me," he said with some conviction. Daisy was listening and reading the article over his shoulder.

"I can't imagine why you took Maria's car in the first place! You could have got a taxi, it would have been less trouble, and less dramatic!" she teased him.

"Jess has been calling me at work, several times, I haven't spoken to her," she was annoyed with her father and Jess for not believing her and not doing anything about what Alex did to Dom. "I don't know what to do, I love Jess and I know she is not to blame but she has a blind side when it comes to my father. Nothing he does is wrong…EVER and it gets tedious, but I have been thinking about ringing her, I miss her." Daisy told Dom her feelings and it made him think about his own parents.

"You must go and see her Daisy, Jess is lovely, she must miss you it isn't her fault what happened. I have been thinking of calling my Papa. I can't stay here forever on my own. You are at work all day, and I have no work. I love being with you, but we need a life, and this is not a good life," he sounded sad as he asked Jess about contacting his family. He had still not told her about Rebecca. Daisy was under the impression that Alex beat Dominic because he was sleeping with her. His obsessive and over-protective control over his precious daughter. She had no idea what the real reason was. Jess had no idea either. Dominic was now in two minds whether to tell her about Rebecca or not. It was weeks and weeks now since the accident on the boat and Daisy had not asked him any more questions, being such a trusting girl, and he was in love with her. She was very special, and he wanted a life with her but with Rebecca hanging over his head, what kind of future could he offer her. The car chase disaster had made him think he needed to get out of there and go back and face the music in Mallorca. His father would help him, and he could tell the truth that it was an accident. He was of good character and had no police record so surely the authorities would be lenient with him, and then maybe he and Daisy could have a life together. He had made up his mind. He would call his parents today, or tomorrow. He would tell Daisy his decision and tell her he may have to go home for a while, but he would be back for her. He could not tell her he loved her. It was not fair on her if he could not promise her a future.

Chapter 20

Dom put the phone down and sat on Daisy's sofa, ashen faced. For the second time in his life he could not move, it was a sensation he hated, and the realisation dawned on him that shock obviously rendered him useless. Perhaps he had been protected from anything that would cause him harm or anxiety as he grew up and his privileged lifestyle in Mallorca certainly contributed to his gentle nature. The last few months had brought him down to earth with a bump and he felt that life would never be the same. He felt happy and safe with Daisy and his only thought now was of her reaction and feelings and not his own.

He had no idea how long he had been sitting there but it was a long time, realising that Daisy would be home in an hour, he forced himself to get up and have a shower, got dressed and waited. He was afraid of her reaction when he told her what had just happened, what he had just heard, and he was scared that she would not only hate him but think even less of Alex than she did right now when he told her.

Daisy went straight to the Old Mill House when her office closed at 5 o'clock. It was unusual to end the day on the dot, but she needed to see Jess and maybe her father. She missed them and needed some answers. Jess was reading when she got there and jumped out of her chair and threw her arms around Daisy, thrilled to see her.

"Oh, this is lovely, I have missed you. I kept ringing your office, but you seemed so busy I knew you would come when you had time," Jess rambled.

"I missed you too Jess, how are you? Where's Dad?"

"He will be back soon, he's been in London for a few days, you know him here one minute, gone the next," she laughed a wry laugh. It seemed all the men in her life spent more time away from her than with her. As she got older this fact dawned on her.

"What did he say about that day Jess?" She would know exactly which day.

"Nothing, really nothing, I asked him, and he just said I didn't need to worry about it, but you wouldn't be seeing him anymore," she recalled the conversation. Alex refused to give her any explanation of why he had hit Dom that day.

"I don't understand Jess, I am twenty five years old, I don't need him fighting for my honour," she laughed then added, "I am not sure why I am laughing, it wasn't funny. He is lucky Dom didn't go to the police and report him for assault!"

"I know, maybe he guessed he wouldn't do that to you, let alone him," Jess tried to placate the situation with a weak excuse.

A car pulled into the driveway of the Old Mill House and Jess felt her heart beat a little faster. It was her father, and she was angry with him. She was more than angry, fuming in fact and even after time had passed since that day she wanted to know why. Time for some honesty.

"Daisy! How are you?" he spoke as if nothing had happened.

"I am actually completely and utterly p**.d off with you and what you did to Dom! I don't understand why you would do that to him and to ME," she stopped herself saying more, she wanted him to explain. She waited.

"Nothing for you to worry about, I hope he has disappeared back where he came from, I told him to sling his hook good and proper, you don't need him in your life Daisy," he looked smug and pleased with himself, like a lion defending his cub. Daisy was even angrier now. He held his arms out to give her a hug, but she shunned the gesture and remained standing rigid, in the same spot.

"You told him to WHAT? Sling his hook, how dare you. I can choose to be with who I like thank you and I don't need you making choices for me," she spat out the words. Her face was thunderous, and he picked up on it. He had never seen her so upset or angry.

"' Woa… stop, I was doing what I thought was best for you, for all of us," he half explained. "He is not good for you Jess, best let this one go."

"This one? What do you mean? What have you got against him? Is there something you are not telling me?" she pushed for more.

"You know nothing about him, and I don't like him, we know nothing about him, and he comes here and suddenly you are together, well I'm not having it," he said which made it sound like an even weaker excuse.

Daisy turned and walked out of the house and got into her car. Jess ran after her and tapped on the window of the car.

"Daisy don't leave like this, please…he means well and loves you, we both do. I can't explain why he is so against Dom.

She wound down the window and grabbed Jess's hand. Jess I love you and him of course but I can't have him dictate my life like this. It was appalling what he did to Dom, and he had no excuse for it. I will ring you. Jess kissed her on the cheek and Daisy drove off, back to Cowes to Dom who was waiting for her.

"Daisy! Oh I've missed you today," he gave her a gin and tonic and asked her to sit down.

"This is nice, why are we drinking very large G & T's? Are we celebrating?" she smiled and sat down.

"I have something to tell you Dom, I went to see Jess on my way home, that's why I am a bit late. It was lovely to see her, she is ok but my father…well, what an idiot. Part of me understands why he did what he did to you, over- protective father blah blah. You are the first real boyfriend I have had, and I think he finds it hard to deal with. Up to now there has just been the three of us and now you come into the equation, and it's thrown him,"

"Did he say anything else?" he asked the question, curious at her sudden forgiveness and ability to justify her father's thinking and make such excuses for him.

"What do you mean? Well, he said he told you to sling your hook and that I didn't need you in my life. How dare he, I am not 14 anymore," she reflected.

"Daisy, I have something to tell you, things I should have told you a long time ago. I know that you know something was not right when we met, and I couldn't tell you. I was scared and ashamed and well Devlin would have killed me if I had told anybody, so I kept it to myself. But today I found out that it will be alright," he stopped and looked at her, waiting for a reaction. He realised she had no idea what he was talking about so continued.

She shrugged her shoulders as if to say, go on then tell me!

"Tell me, I know there is something Dom, what is it?" she said with some frustration in her voice.

"I am glad you have been to see Jess and your father, but I am shocked he didn't tell you the truth," he poured himself another drink and stood by the window, Jess got up and joined him, she opened the double doors that led to the balcony and sat down. He sat opposite her, a small table decorated with blue and white mosaic tiles between them. They both needed some air, and it was warm and sunny out there, but refreshing with the slight sea breeze that came in from the Solent. It was a perfect evening, and the view was, as usual, busy and interesting.

"Hear me out before you react Daisy, because you may feel that you can't accept what happened and I am still scared you will think badly of me when I have to said all this, promise you will think about it before you reject me?"

She couldn't believe what he was saying – 'reject me' what on earth was he going to tell her?

"Reject you? Why would I do that? Surely it can't be that bad?" She held her breath.

"Devlin and I have been business partners for the best part of ten years, we shared an apartment, but our relationship has been poor for the last year or so. I was very young when it started and I thought that was what I wanted, in the end it wasn't. I don't know why we stayed together but we did, for the business mainly, probably being too busy and too lazy to do anything about it. I came here with Devlin, but I wasn't supposed to," he took a breath and looked at her, trying to detect any reaction to what he had just told her.

"Go on, don't stop, I knew something wasn't right with you and Devlin, I just couldn't put my finger on it," she chipped in, encouraging him to continue.

"He stole my father's yacht, that is the first thing that happened. I don't really know why he stole it, except he wanted to come to England, and over the months I have had time to think about that. The conclusion I came to was that he must have had a good reason not to go by the normal route, fly or ferry to avoid the authorities. I think he is mixed up in some serious stuff. Those people at The Copse are not good people Daisy, God knows what they are plotting and planning," he paused as if organising events in his head, he paced up and down as he finished telling the story.

"Anyway, as I said, he stole my father's yacht. I was on board with a girl I had met some weeks before, we were… erm, you know… in the cabin below and realised the boat was moving," he stopped talking, she was taking it in and saying nothing, he continued, his anger rising visibly.

"B*.tard, stealing my families yacht! After everything they did for him for years, I was shocked and confronted him on deck, he shoved me, I was so angry, and I hit him several times…" he took a deep breath.

"As I swung my arm to hit him again I hit this girl, Rebecca, we both heard the crack as my elbow hit her in the face. She was behind me, and I didn't know. I didn't see her behind me. Well, she went overboard," he stopped when Daisy spoke.

"Oh my God Dom, why didn't you tell me all this before? Is the girl alright?"

"We thought she was dead, all this time we thought she was dead, we couldn't find her. But he wouldn't stop the boat, we threw life belts over the side, but he wouldn't stop. I was screaming at him to stop but he wouldn't listen. He said I had murdered her and if I didn't keep my mouth shut I would be blamed for her death. That's why I couldn't say anything or go home; I know now I should have just told somebody, but he wouldn't let me," he was relieved to have finally told her, he waited for her reaction.

"I don't know what to s…" she started to speak, she was clearly shocked, and he stopped her mid-sentence.

"It's ok, she is ok. She is alive. I found out this afternoon. All this time I thought I had killed somebody. I rang my father and he told me, they found her, a miracle, some fishing boat picked her up! She was in hospital for a long time, lost her memory but it came back, and she told them it was an accident. But Jess that is not the worst part of this. Prepare yourself for an even bigger shock," he looked at her, she was shaking.

"What could be worse that some poor girl going overboard in the middle of the ocean?" she asked. Shocked at all of this, but at least the severity of it all made sense now. No wonder he was a shell when she met him, it sounded enough to tip the strongest person over the edge. She felt enormous relief this girl, whoever she was is ok and Dom was not going to be blamed for her death.

"Jess your father knew, when he attacked me, he knew,"

"He knew what?" now she was confused.

"He went to Mallorca, my home, he went to see my parents to tell them this girl was ok. He found her in the hospital and went to tell my parents I was safe and told them the story. They know it was an accident, your father knows it was an accident and yet when he came back from telling my parents he attacked me and told me to keep away from you, I don't understand, it was an accident," he looked drained and looked at her.

"I am even more confused now, think about it, he went to see your parents about a girl who had gone overboard? How did he make the link with you? Did she know your parents?" it was a perfectly sensible question.

"I think my papa said something about your father was investigating some people and he couldn't say any more," even that sounded ridiculous to Dom. "I see what you mean, so who was he investigating? Wasn't me, I haven't done anything, so must have been Devlin. Oh my God she must have got close to me to get to him. She did ask me a lot of questions about him." He stopped to think.

"That means he is investigating Devlin, it must be if it isn't you. Who else did you mix with?"

"Nobody really, just us two always, and she had come on the scene a few weeks before, she approached me, wouldn't leave me alone, wherever I went, she was there! It all fits now," he sat back in his chair as if exhausted by it all.

Her face was evil, he had never ever seen her look that way, so angry she looked as if she would explode with anger. Her face was fixed in a deathly white rage, her eyes were almost bulging out of her head. She couldn't speak, noises seemed to be coming from her mouth, but she was incoherent, nothing he could understand for a couple of minutes.

"Please tell me that rage is not aimed at me!" he used his most seductive gentle voice to ask the question, he was dreading the answer.

"I, I, I don't know what to do Dom, how could he do this to me, to you, to us, what do I do, tell me. I want to kill him, I love him but this, this...this is beneath contempt. I hate him, I hate him. Please God tell me Jess doesn't know about this, please give me one parent who is not evil."

He held her for a long time, she just sobbed and sobbed then relaxed and he looked at her. She wiped her eyes and seemed to be calmer. He made her sit down and he sat beside her.

"I am ok honestly I am. Just a shock. Mallorca? Is that were you are from? I have always wanted to go there..."

"I must go home Daisy, my father is sending a private jet to Sandown airport to pick me up. He will bring my passport as I don't have it, you know I have nothing. Will you be ok? Will you wait for me? Say you will wait for me Daisy," he had hope in his heart and was praying she would agree.

"Of course I will wait for you, it is such a relief to know what happened. I think I need some time to get my head around all of this. I will take a bit of leave, they can manage without me for a couple of weeks. I have tried to imagine the hold Devlin had over you, I never imagined it would be this. You are not safe here for sure Dom, go and I will be here. My father is another matter, I don't know what to do about him," she was beside herself with an angry feeling of grief where he was concerned. It was a new experience not to hold her father on the highest pedestal as she had all her life. "My one hope is that Jess had no idea about all that stuff on the boat and will help me get to the bottom of it all."

Chapter 21

"Two MILLION, you gave them TWO MILLION!!!!!?" Devlin was pacing up and down the office. The Russian had returned, and they all gathered in the office.

"What do you mean you gave them two million? How did you give them two million? Where did you get two million?" he could not stop saying two million. "Two million," he said it again.

It was a staggering amount of money, where did Nikolai Markarov get two million pounds to give to the Cartels? If he had access to that much money why was he involved in this. His head was racing and nothing tangible was emerging.

Nikolai looked pleased with himself and more than glad to be back on cool English soil after the heat of the Cartel's red ranch and the meetings with those gun toting New Mexicans. This all seemed so calm and organised. Devlin was not going to believe his story, so he had to come up with something, or nothing. If he could get away with not explaining then he would do just that, explain nothing.

They were meeting to welcome Nikolai back and agree on tighter security around The Copse after the car chase that nearly cost Dominic Montpelier his life. Devlin was beside himself that he had disappeared, he had people out looking for him, but he had vanished off the face of the earth. He knew those men in the Daimler were not after Dom, and that it must be his new wife who was in danger here.   She owed the rival Cartel money and word was out by now that she was out and back in business.

"Nobody goes out on their own. We all need close protection and I have obtained weapons for all of us.   Theo is in charge of Security, and he will be responsible for putting extra staff in the grounds for the time being. They know where we are now and need to be ready for anything. We come with baggage and these people don't forget. They will be even angrier now those two goons are dead.   So I say it again, NOBODY goes out alone, take one of the armed men with you, even to the supermarket," he slammed his fist on the desk, to wake them all up and to get his point across.

"Who do you think it was in the Daimler?" a simple but poignant question from Theo…

"My guess is the Cartel from El Paso or some of the people Matt Hayward ripped off, they have been waiting for Maria's release. She is surprised they didn't try to get to her in prison, but they kept a pretty good eye on her, and she was careful, so we have to imagine they won't give up, Theo, you will brief us on anything that comes up. Cameras are going up tomorrow and the security system on the house is being upgraded this week. It is five years old and some of us can get through it…" he looked at Jamal as he spoke and smiled. There will be 24 hour surveillance on the property from tonight.

"Serious stuff my friend," responded the Russian.

"It is indeed and now to some more serious stuff… two million? Explain please, I think I need to sit down for this one," commented Devlin who couldn't wait for the reasons for this amount of money that had apparently changed hands. He aimed his question at the Russian, Nikolai Markarov.

"We got the deal, that is all you need to know and when it's done, and the money is in I get the two mill back" he was confident in his reply.

Devlin was not going to give up.

"I need more than that, we need more than that, was it your own money? We need details. There has to be some trust here we are dealing with the big boys, and I am no push over… spill!"

"Why that much? Is that normal?" he was clutching at straws, he had no idea how these things worked. He looked like a woodpecker, pecking on the giant wooden gates of hell, and getting nowhere.

Maria interrupted, saving her new husband's honour. He really was an idiot if he thinks you can just go to a place like New Mexico and expect them to cough up drugs in the mass amount they were asking for and do it without some kind of security deposit. What a star this Russian is to do that and so early in their relationship. She was impressed and said so.

"So Mr Russian, congratulations. You got out alive! Many

don't as we know. Devlin darling he has done well, and we will find out about the money another time, in private. I want to know, and I want details, so please let us concentrate on the detail here. This deal is massive, and we not only have that to contend with now we have God knows who trying to blow us to bits to stop us or scare us or both. Whatever it is we have work to do. Theo, get going with the new staff and Jamal I want to talk to you about logistics. Nikolai, you and I will talk later over a vodka or two. We need to raise a glass to your success," Maria was firing on all her cylinders and Devlin was impressed and quietly pleased that he had married her, so she was on his side. She knew what she was doing. He did not. That was the truth of it, he was out of his depth, but he had to give the illusion that he was in control or look stupid. Maria already felt he was stupid after his poor performance in front of the team, which was not a place he needed to be.

Chapter 22

Maria was damned if she did and damned if she didn't. Her performance in the meeting today was a taster of the old Maria, back in control and in charge. She knew exactly what needed doing because she had years of experience. To make Devlin look stupid or let him waffle on, a decision had to be made and she hoped she hadn't gone in too strong. Devlin laughed at her once because she mentioned the cave on Chale beach was stocked with food and dry clothes, but somebody had to be practical. A lot of men would be involved in this heist if it was to be successful. They needed somewhere to stay the night before, they needed feeding and they needed transport. In the old house they had the secret wing with metal army beds, here they would need sleeping bags, and basic sleeping arrangements. If she didn't think for them then nobody would. Success would be in the detail. Small boats had been hired to pick up all the goods off the tankers and then more to take the goods from the beach and take them all over the country and to France and Belgium. Men didn't do practical, a well fed army worked better. She would make sure it went like clockwork with the help of Jamal.

"Well that went well, apart from the two million. Where did that come from? We need to know. Is it his own money or is somebody bankrolling him? Important questions need to be asked. Jamal will find out for us, they respect him. I don't want lies and platitudes from the Russian. I have this feeling he will lie, I can smell it a mile off," she took a long drink from her glass and put it down on the desk. There was no more time to talk, the alarm that had been installed this week on the perimeter fence was going off. There were people in the grounds, Theo was alerted and went out with three others, going through their routine search of the old stable block and outbuildings.

Devlin told Maria to stay where she was, and he left her in the balcony bedroom.

"Stay away from the window and lock this door," he instructed and closed the door behind him.

There was a panic room just off the balcony room, so if the alert went off she could double lock herself in there. She prayed that would not happen and it was a false alarm. It was lined with metal and had supplies in there, so in case of trouble anybody could survive in there for a few days. She had thought of everything when the house was rebuilt. Knowing there might be trouble from South America.

There had already been one attempt on her life, they were not after Dom. He had no enemies as far as they knew, and long discussions led them to come to the conclusion that it was Maria they were after. Security had been tightened and The Copse was as much like a fortress as they could make it. They had a 24 hour guard all around the grounds, that were not extensive but big enough for people to be able to hide and come in without being seen. There was no boundary wall, just a wire fence between the house, the woods and open countryside. Devlin was castigating himself for using this house as their HQ, maybe they should have gone somewhere more secure.

"We are sitting f.**k..g ducks here with all this glass and the open land," he said to Theo over the radio. "Keep me in the loop if you see anything, over," he clicked the button, and the radio was silent.

The gunshots reverberated through the woods and Jess and Alex heard them and ran to lock their doors, avoiding the windows. It was instinct. They had never forgotten the sound of the gunshot inside their house ten years ago and they just heard three shots.

"Is that what I think it is?" asked Jess, out of breath after running to lock the back door. She slumped in front of the sofa and told Alex to sit on the floor with her, but he had other ideas.

"I'm going out to see what's going on," he told Jess

"No you are NOT," she was very firm in her demand, "Don't you dare leave me here on my own," it seemed to do the trick.

They sat on the floor together, he put his arm around her and reassured her it was probably just a car backfiring. They were super sensitive to any kind of gunshot type noise, and she agreed reluctantly and snuggled into his shoulder.

"This is cosy," he laughed.

"Well I wouldn't say cosy exactly, maybe a tad uncomfortable?" She dragged a few cushions off the sofa onto the floor as she spoke.

He kissed her on the top of her head, and she looked up at him, that wonderful smile of his radiated. How could she be in danger with this man beside her? He was as beautiful as they day she met him, his hair was going slightly grey at the edges now, but his eyes still sparkled, his skin was tanned, and no wrinkles had dared to show. She wanted to touch him all the time, but not here on this floor at this moment. There was just this safe business that was still bothering her. There it was, right in front of them behind that panel. It was at eye level, they were ten feet away from it. Should she mention it? What on earth would he say. How could she go on for the rest of her life not knowing?

Back at The Copse it was bedlam, two shots were fired towards the house from deep in the woods beyond the lane. One caught one of the windows at the bottom of the building and Theo fired back, one shot, he was sure he hit him and watched him limp away, through the telescopic viewfinder on the rifle.

Whoever it was got away on a fast motor bike, they heard it roar away into the distance. When he was sure there was nobody else out there, they edged their way up to where the intruder had been, and found blood on the ground, so he was right – he did hit whoever was out there.

"They are trying to scare us," Devlin was trying to be calm. "We showed them we are prepared, so hopefully it will put them off any future attempts, we will have to be vigilant," he looked worried, despite his convincing speech.

September 1st was approaching fast. Apart from a few squabbles inhouse it was all going well. The Russian and Theo were deep in conversation and Maria's sharp ears alerted her to more than the English language.

They stopped talking when she came close and shouted to her "Hey Maria, have you got vodka in this place?" they were laughing as they teased her.

"We need more than vodka today, have you seen Devlin?" she demanded. "I can't find him anywhere?"

She was seething and worried about news from Jamal about the 2 million that had been given to the Cartel in New Mexico. He came back with this information and now she had no idea what to do with it. Was it good news or bad? His relationship with these people in New Mexico was rock solid so she believed every word that had come back…diamonds. He paid them in f*…g diamonds! How? Her brain was like a vast array of cogs clicking into place, and it kept coming back to not knowing a damn thing about the Russian. Who the hell was he? She was so used to being in control and knowing when her people sneezed this was not lying well with her. Did Devlin know more than he was letting on? Jamal brought him here and yet he was shocked when he found out and told her the news.

"How the hell has he got hold of two mill in diamonds?" Jamal was as gobsmacked as she was when she heard him say it. She had to think and think fast. Who was playing who here? She had grave concerns over the team that was in place, the logistics were now pretty much sorted, but this collection of staff was such an unknown she was more than concerned. Jamal seemed to be the only one she trusted. Even Devlin was unsettling her. He seemed at a loss. No substance to him, that was how she was thinking. He talked the talk but when it came to actually having ideas or having any kind of authority he was like chocolate in the sun… he just melted away and let others come in and claimed their ideas for himself. She noticed this tactic more and more and was not fooled by it. What was the point of him? His only saving grace was the way he looked, and he was being very attentive to her lately, so she would not get rid of him yet.

Theo was surprising her daily, he was so protective of everybody and had ideas way above his paygrade. Somehow she felt safer in his company than all the others. He exuded strength from every pore. He was too young for her which was a shame, but she considered it… a small nag inside her head made her think it was a move too far and she had seen him looking at Devlin so maybe barking up a wrong tree. So she left it.

Glynis.M.Parkes

Chapter 23

Daisy was lonely. Dominic had been gone for three days and this time off work she planned for herself, a break to get her head together, was having the opposite effect. The apartment had never felt so empty, Dom had left such a void in her life which was a new experience for Daisy. She missed him like crazy. He phoned her several times a day and always at night before she went to sleep, flowers arrived that morning, but it wasn't the same as having him there.

Jess was up in London meeting with her old business partner Harry. She reluctantly agreed to the idea to rekindle that partnership after years of him nagging to do another collection with her for Paris fashion week. Despite her protestations he would not let it go and so she agreed to go up and speak to him, she might think about it. Now Daisy had left home, and was looking like a permanent thing, lately Alex always seemed busy, she needed a new challenge.

Daisy had no desire to see her father, it had been a while since she had seen him, she was too angry after what he did to Dom and that anger didn't appear to be going away; he had never given her a reason for it, but she missed him pure and simple. Maybe she would go up to the Old Mill House today. Jess rang her at the weekend and told her about the gunshots they had heard but nothing since so she could go with that as the excuse, to see if they were ok.

When she got there the house seemed quiet. Alex's car was in the drive, so she let herself in through the front door. Normally she would shout out 'hello,' or 'is anybody here,' but for some reason she didn't this time. Probably because she wasn't feeling very cheery at the thought of seeing Alex, so she walked through the house, looking into rooms but there was no sign of her father.

She heard voices in the garden, loud voices and laughter, raucous laughter. Quietly she went to the kitchen and carefully looked through the window, hardly believing her own eyes…sitting at the table in the garden was her father deep in conversation with a big chap with black and white striped hair. Who was he? She had no idea. They were having an intense discussion and it was not in English. It felt as if she was watching a stranger, well two strangers. Was that Russian they were speaking? Not only speaking they were laughing like old friends and drinking vodka, making gestures of celebration, clinking glasses, clearly pleased about something. Panic set in, what to do? Should she go out and say hello or slip away and ask Jess, taking her chance to get out of there she swiftly left the kitchen, went back down the hallway and out of the front door. She was pleased she had left her car at the bottom of the drive facing the gate, so hopefully they would not hear her start the car, thanking God hers was a quiet car she drove away down the lane unseen and unheard. Would she be able to wait until Jess came back? No she would ring her as soon as she got back to the apartment.

"Jess?" it was a bad line so she couldn't hear her very well.

"Yes who is that?" asked Jess.

"It's me Daisy," she laughed.

"Daisy…are you ok? Is everything alright?" she asked, concerned because Daisy hardly ever rang her these days.

"Jess, the weirdest thing just happened. I went to the house and Dad was in the garden with this huge chap with the wildest hair, black and white stripes, is the only way I can describe it. Who is he? I don't know him, do you?"

"No, I don't think so, maybe it was somebody from his work," she was not concerned at all.

"Jess, the thing is…right, a question. Does Dad speak another language? Because I have never heard him speak anything other than English, he couldn't even help me with my French homework," she remembered.

"I know," Jess laughed. "Why are you asking? Do you need to translate something?"

"No no, nothing like that, I went into the house and stood in the kitchen watching Dad and this bloke in the garden, they were drinking vodka and celebrating something."

"Well Dad is allowed to drink Daisy!" Jess laughed.

"Yes I know that, but they were speaking to each other in another language, I think it was Russian!" she waited.

"Russian? Surely not, are you sure? No I've never heard him speak any other language, Daisy are you sure? If you were in the kitchen? Maybe the radio was on?" She couldn't believe what Daisy was saying.

"No the radio wasn't on Jess, they were having a real conversation and it was Russian. Not French, not German, not Spanish, it was Russian, I am stunned, when are you back? I need to see you, I can't deal with this it's weird."

"I'll be back tomorrow, and I will come to Cowes, I'll come straight there, before lunch, don't say anything to your Dad, we need to think about this!"

"Ok, see you tomorrow," and they hung up.

Secret safe, now a different language, what was going on? It felt surreal, ten years ago Jess witnessed some odd things happening, Alex was kidnapped from the Old Mill House, and nobody ever really explained that incident, she saw him fighting with Matt Hayward, but he denied knowing him. She accepted both were mistaken identity, but where they? Apart from Matt being shot inside the house, since that time nothing out of the ordinary had happened to them, and now these two things one after the other. Was it that she had not noticed? His job was not 9 – 5 and his routine was non-existent, so life was always irregular and unplanned, two days were never the same in a row. Maybe there was more, and she just hadn't noticed. She needed to speak to Maria, something in her head was

WIGHT DIAMONDS & CRAZY RED DOGS

nagging at her…something she heard her say about having French and Russians in the house. Was she imagining that? Jess was sharp when it came to remembering things, not so much when it came to Alex and the rosy glow that she saw around him.

Chapter 24

There he was, just as Daisy described him, huge man with black and white striped hair. Jess could see him through the enormous window at the front of the house. The next few minutes would confirm if he was Russian.

"Jess! This is a nice surprise," Maria welcomed Jess to The Copse.

Theo answered the door and invited her in, with the usual double peck on each cheek. She blushed, quite liking that little double kissing ritual.

"Are you busy?" Jess asked Maria.

"I am always busy, but always have time for you," Maria replied and indicated they go into the kitchen. Since somebody took a pot shot at the house they had all stopped going into the garden which would have been preferable.

"Can we talk, I think I have a problem," Jess was so pleased to be able to offload her concerns about Alex and Maria was the only person she could go to. Opening her mouth to ask about the Russian, he suddenly appeared like a Genie popping out of a lamp, as if being summoned him. His timing was perfect but stopped Jess in her tracks. The description Daisy had given her was so accurate there was no mistaking the black and white striped hair. Maria stopped talking and introduced him to Jess.

"Jess this is Nikolai, Nikolai Markarov, Nik this is Jess, she lives next door."

"Pleasure to meet you at last," he kissed her hand which threw her a bit and she blushed.

"Nikolai? That sounds Russian!" she took her chance to ask.

"Correct, I am from Moscow, you are very clever young lady."

Jess was hanging on his every word and yes he did say 'pleasure to meet you at last...'at last'... You only say that if you have heard of the person. A small comment but huge on implication. It was all pointing to Alex knowing him and talking about her or Maria had mentioned her.

"Come on, the office is empty," she realised the embarrassment from the hand kissing thing and pulled her away from him and took her upstairs to the room with the glass balcony closing the door behind them. She checked the bathroom was empty and the panic room was locked.

Maria pulled the chairs away from the window, explaining that it wasn't wise to be on show right now. Jess resisted the urge to ask her about the gunshots she and Alex had heard a few nights before, but Maria was telling her that it was not safe to stand in full sight on that balcony.

How to start this conversation was the difficult bit, but Maria had been thinking about the safe and they seemed to flow into it with no awkwardness   at all.

"Tell me about your Russian friend Maria, I am curious, he is a handsome fellow, all that hair, so unusual," she laughed but glad to have an opening sentence. "Have you ever mentioned me to him?"

"Erm, don't think so why?" Jess didn't respond to that one.

The first question threw Maria because she didn't know that much about him. A man living in her house whose background was sketchy to say the least but seemed to know what he was doing and had pulled off a huge deal with a major Cartel in Albuquerque. What could she say, definitely not mention the upcoming consignment on September 1st for sure. What else did she know, next to nothing? She knew Jess was not the kind of person to ask questions and to respect Maria's privacy. All those years ago when Maria lived on her own at The Copse, and operated her office from there, Jess was a regular visitor, but never once did she ask about any of it. She didn't even seem interested, not in the slightest.

"Sorry about this, we are having some security issues here right now, the car chase thing and the other night we thought somebody out there hunting took a pot shot at us, so we are being extra vigilant, probably nothing but you can't be too careful eh?" she explained but wasn't all that convincing.

"Drink?" she offered Jess a drink from the cabinet in the corner of the room, but she declined.

"No thanks, bit early for me, look I wanted to ask you about the Russian chap because Daisy said he was at my house yesterday talking to Alex in the garden. We are totally thrown by that, do you know why he was over at my house? Did you send him to ask Alex something? I know I can trust you Maria and you can trust me...this goes no further. I don't want to ask Alex because frankly, I don't think he would tell me, especially if it is work related," she waited for Maria to respond. The look on her face said it all, she was as surprised as Jess.

"Wow! Really? He was at your house? What the...I have no idea, I can ask Devlin, he needs to hear this, he might have an idea. If he has then he certainly hasn't shared it with me, I don't know what to say Jess. That has thrown me! What on earth would Nikolai be doing talking to Alex? That is so random! We need to find out and quick." Maria shot out of the room and down the stairs, finding Devlin in the kitchen she asked him to join her and Jess upstairs, she was out of breath when she returned.

"Right, Jess tell Devlin, I trust him with this, he needs to know, and we need to find out," she sat down.

"I can't see the link at all! What were they talking about? Do you know?" Devlin was also surprised as he asked Jess.

"I don't want to panic and think he is telling Alex about what we are doing business wise! They would not be as open as meeting at yours Jess surely? But we don't know until we know, and I will find out," he sounded determined.

"I don't know what they were talking about, Daisy saw them through the window, they were in the garden, speaking in Russian which upset her, and I understand that, must have been an odd experience! We have never heard him speak any other language but English, so Russian! It really shocked her. She got out of there before they realised she was watching them through the window, she left the house and went home. She wasn't going to stay to find out."

"Jess, look leave this with us, we will do some digging and see what we can find out. I agree it is odd and we need to find out. It could be nothing, but we can't take that risk! We have some business going on right now and it's at a very delicate stage. Anything that rocks the boat wouldn't be good for us. Will you ask Alex about it?"

Jess shook her head, "No, I don't think I want to tell him that Daisy saw him, not because he was with your Russian friend, but speaking the language, I don't think I want to know," Jess confirmed. "I like the quiet life, and this would be major confrontation for me and Alex, and I really don't want that."

"Just as I thought, no, and probably best if you don't," Maria agreed with her.

"Jess, I know I asked you before, but when all of that stuff happened, just after I went to prison, did Alex act in a different way?" she was probing and hoping for some chink of a clue.

"What do you mean act in a different way?" Jess was confused, it was ten years ago. "I don't think so, in what way? I can't remember!"

"It's so hard for me to ask you but what about money? Did he seem to have more money than usual? God I hate asking you that, bloody cheek, forget I asked," she had to ask.

Jess looked at her and then at Devlin, what should she say. Ten years is a long time, but she knew what they were asking. Things she had buried in silence all that time. The new stables he had built, the horses, the apartment he bought for Daisy, new cars, putting endless money into her business. She felt herself get very hot and uncomfortable and suddenly needed to get out of there. What was Maria telling her? That Alex was involved in things he shouldn't? It was obvious but she didn't understand at the same time. The safe, that bloody safe. They needed to see inside it.

'Can we open the safe?' it was in her head, but she couldn't say it.

"Look I'll speak to you tomorrow, I've got a really bad headache," and with that she flew out of the house.

"I will ring you if we get to the bottom of it," Maria shouted after Jess as she ran down the stairs.

"We need to open that safe," she said to Devlin, forgetting

she had not even mentioned it to him.   He asked her to repeat what she just said.

That hidden safe was playing on her mind day after day. She needed to know what was inside it. The 2 million in diamonds had been popping into her head over and over as well. Nobody had pressed Nikolai to explain that. They were all a little afraid of him and that was ridiculous, and she had not wanted to mention it in front of Devlin just yet. Something had occurred to her during one of her contemplations, maybe the safe and the diamonds were linked, Jess had just come in and said Alex and the Russian were meeting. Was it all coincidence? Maria knew about coincidence but knew that gut instinct was stronger than coincidence.   She did see a lot of velvet bags in that safe, and velvet bags usually meant jewellery, she had had enough of it in her life. She spent long hours just thinking things through. Maybe because she had trained herself to do that in prison. Thinking whiled away the hours then and sometimes now when nothing was happening in their rural hideaway she sat on her own with the cogs whirring in her head. It was either as mad as a bag of frogs in there with phones ringing all day long or nothing, waiting… and they were waiting for the 1st of September and the two tankers coming into Chale Bay with the goods on board.

"What safe Maria? Whose safe? You said we need to open the safe," he asked her three times before she replied.

"There is a safe," she took a deep breath. She wasn't going to tell him everything just yet. "I am going to ask you a question Dev, do you know anybody who could open a safe, a big safe? And if you do not then we need to persuade the owner of that safe to open it," she was being obtuse, and Devlin picked up on it.

"Persuade?" he laughed.

"It's not funny, this is serious Dev, we may need to use a bit of 'friendly' persuasion if you know what I mean," she pulled a face that said, you know exactly what I mean.

"Tell me who owns the safe, you can't just say something like that and leave it, tell me. I need details, where is it? In a bank? A house? What kind of safe? And why do we need to open it by force did you say?" he was bemused by the dilemma.

"That's not a problem is it? We have the man power and I have to trust that you know what you are doing," she was speaking, and he was beyond curious. "Let me sleep on it, it might be nothing." Maria was trying to avoid any more questions about the safe.

Should she tell him the whole story of the safe? It was a bit late to worry about trusting him. She married him but still there were some doubts. He had done nothing to make her distrust him since they got together, but still there was something. Maybe something about his life or his past he was not telling her. She would sleep on it.

"I am concerned about the Russian being next door, what is that all about? Alex is MI5 or something Official, and our Russian is deep in conversation with him, should we be worried? Do we ask him? We might have a problem, we have three weeks before Chale Bay, this is no time for sides to be crossing over. What do we do?" she was worried and for now Devlin was distracted by the Nikolai problem. She would talk to Jess again about the safe and think about telling Devlin what she saw in the safe.

Chapter 25

The gun was pointed at Nikolai's head. Devlin meant business and had come into the room behind Nikolai who was sprawled on the sofa as if he didn't have a care in the world. Devlin was behind him with a hand on his shoulder, pushing him back down when he tried to get up.

"Tell me why you were next door with Alex McFarlane, you have one chance, and I want the truth," Devlin demanded an answer. There was nobody else in the house, he made sure of that by sending them all down to Chale to mingle like visitors to see the beach, the landing ground and the caves for themselves.

Nikolai said nothing for a few minutes then held his hands up as if to say, ok I give in, let me get up and said so.

"Let me sit u…"

"No, stay exactly where you are, tell me, and I will only ask you one more time, why were you next door speaking to Alex?"

"I was walking and bumped into him, he invited me round when I said I didn't know many people here, we were just having a drink like old friends, why are you asking? How dare you point a f *…g gun at me, who do you think you are?" He was treating the threat from Devlin with counter threat back at him.

"I am paying your f*…g wages you idiot, that's who I am and speaking to him next door is not alright, do you hear? He is MI5 for God's sake," he was angry.

"I was being normal with him you idiot, showing him we are not afraid of him, right under his nose, just being friendly, it is you who are the idiot," he struggled and resisted the hand on his shoulder, forcing Dev away from him, he sat up calling Devlin's bluff. Dev put the gun away and repeated his point.

"Do NOT speak to him next door, do you hear me? He is trouble, trust me, he comes across as one of the boys, but he is dangerous to us," he was shouting at Nikolai but felt none of it was going in. He walked out of the room and ran upstairs to the office. Nikolai smiled, 'if only you knew my friend, if only you knew.'

"We need to talk," Devlin closed the door behind him, standing with his back to the door, almost in defiance, body language saying you are not leaving this room until I have some answers...

"The safe? Something is not right here Maria, what are you not telling me?" Devlin was angry and pumped up from his encounter with the Russian.

 Maria just stared at him. Crunch time, she had no choice but to include him in the discussions she had been having with Jess. To share what she knew about the safe, and her conclusions, right or wrong. She had no-one else to confide in. Jamal was not someone she would want to know about the safe, his son, not in a million years, and Nikolai, well he might be part of the problem. So this was it, Devlin needed to know. It would be interesting to get his take on things anyway. In her head she was piecing things together, Nikolai and the diamonds, where did they come from? A ridiculous situation because they had no idea, he was refusing to tell them. Alex conversing with him in Russian, why? The safe full of money in Jess's house. She took a deep breath and told him to sit down, she wished Jess was there, she had not had a chance to speak to her again, but she would as soon as this was over.

"I have just had five minutes with Nikolai," he said as he sat down on one of the big black leather chairs.

"And?" Maria was curious but not convinced he had any answers, and she was right.

"And, and? And I am more than mad now Maria, tell me about this safe. Now!"

"Says he bumped into him, and they were just having a friendly coffee, well he said drink, or words to that effect. "I don't believe him."

"No, neither do I, we need to get to the bottom of this diamond business. Have you asked him about that again?" she doubted he had and wondered why she had bothered to ask.

"No again, I have asked Jamal and he doesn't think the Russian has a spare bean to his name, so somebody is bankrolling him, but why?"

"I think 'how' is the question, yes 'why' but 'how' might answer the 'why'…" she paused to gather her thoughts. How to word this, it was important she got it right.

"The safe…" Devlin said it again.

"When I got to the Old Mill House after the fire…" she gulped as if the whole experience encased her again. "After what happened to Matt…" she was finding this more difficult that she ever imagined.

"No, let me start again. I am under the impression you think I have the money that Matt skimmed of this Organisation in 69. Be honest with me Devlin. I know you have asked me in jest, but I think, you do think I have it. I am telling you now, I don't have that money. I think Matt thought I had it, which is why he did what he did to me. That much is clear in my head. He went to the bank vault in Zurich to take out that money and it was gone, way before the Chale bay heist and way before I shot him, I think he blamed me for the empty box, but it wasn't me who took it all," she stopped to take in the expression on Devlin's face. A face of a man who had married a woman for her money and found out she had none. She could see it.

"Wow! I had no idea, why didn't you tell me all this before?" he was shocked. "Do you think that is why he tried to kill you in the fire?" It was all making sense now. A reason for Matts erratic attack on Maria.

"Before what? Before you married me? Well too late now, but all is not lost. Listen to me," she demanded his attention that had obviously flagged in the last two minutes. Bloody man, all he is interested in is my f*…g money. She was right. Right there it showed in his face, but no time for that now, he was here, they were married, and he was her only hope of dealing with this safe business, no matter how disappointed he was.

"When I went to the Old Mill House and shot Matt, Alex threw me on the sofa and took the gun off me. He put that gun up high on a shelf so I couldn't reach it. He also took a gun off his daughter! I was watching him, and he put THAT gun in a safe in the living room, right in front of me. Jess knew nothing about that safe until I mentioned it to her recently and she was as shocked as you look, more so in fact."

"His daughter? Daisy? My God she must have been a child, what was she doing with a gun? A real gun?" he sounded shocked.

"Yes a real gun, that is immaterial, and I have no idea why she had it, but listen to me," she was getting frustrated with the length of this explanation.

"Ok, so there is a safe in the house next door, so what?" he was completely nonplussed about this revelation.

"If I tell you that the safe was full, and I mean FULL of money and stuffed velvet bags and he had trouble finding a space to put the gun, would that make you interested?" she finished speaking and watched his face change shape. He didn't know what to say at first, but his instinct told him she may have something here. His ears pricked up when she said stuffed velvet bags.

"So, you want to have a look inside? But it was ten years ago Maria, that money will be long gone. Velvet bags…" he said it but didn't finish the sentence.

"What do you suggest? "he asked her.

"We use some strong arm stuff and make Alex open it. We have the man power and we have weapons, he wouldn't need to know it was us," she was telling him to use force on Alex.

He started to laugh and laughed and laughed. He was beside himself with the irony of what he was listening to.

"I need a drink, have we got any beer up here? No, on second thoughts Vodka, neat, big one and I suggest you have one too," he sat and watched her pour them both very large shots of vodka and she slammed his down in front of him, she was upset and that was not lost on him.

"Why are you laughing? Don't laugh at me, it's not funny, I saw what I saw. Jess isn't saying if Alex had money ten years ago, but they live a good life and all that costs…"

"I think it is time for me to come clean with you dear wife…

if ever there was a time for sharing this is it, are you sitting comfortably?" Before he could finish the sentence she threw a book at him.

"You are the most infuriating human being... what do you mean it is time for you to come clean?" She had no idea what he was talking about which annoyed her. Usually astute pre-empting conversations came naturally to her, but not this one, what was he going to confess? It sounded as if he was about to confess...

Chapter 26

It was August 30th, 1979, exactly ten years since the last Chale Bay drugs and weapons drop on the beach. The Copse was full of people, men in rooms upstairs, the beach crew, brought in at the dead of night and by the back door. The crew that would lift off the goods from the two tankers in the bay on the 1st and 2nd of September. They would go out the same way late evening of the 1st of September for the big one. They were all ready. Tempers were short as they tried to fill the hours, and the drinks were long, men who normally would not drink and had planned and trained for this day under the guidance of Devlin and Theo, were all having a few tonight to remember the last time they were all together, the heist that worked like clockwork but ended in disaster when they were shopped by somebody, and everything was confiscated. It would not happen again. They were determined, especially knowing the rewards would be double what they would have made out of it ten years ago.

Jamal and Theo had dotted all the I's and crossed all the T's they could find so now it was just a waiting game. The only problem would be the weather that was forecast fine, but a storm was expected later in the week. They were watching the skies and praying for a calm sea at the weekend.

Next door at the Old Mill House Jess was anxious as Alex had not been seen for three days. They had had no word from him and even

Daisy was worried. Things had not been good between them for weeks since the Dom fight that had not been resolved and left father and daughter estranged for the first time in her life. Daisy was getting closer and closer to Dom, he rang her every day and had flown over to see her every weekend since he left, they met in a hotel but kept it quiet and told nobody where they were meeting. Jess thought they met in London, but Daisy didn't tell her just to be sure. If Jess didn't know then she could say in all honesty that she had no idea which was the truth. That was how they played it and both women were happy with that. Daisy rang Jess to let her know she was ok so that put Jess at ease, knowing she was happy and safe.

Dominic's father had spoken to the Spanish police, and they were quite satisfied there were no charges to be made against his son. He was not in charge of the boat, and they would not be pursuing him at all. They may go after Devlin but would not discuss it further, It had been hanging over him for weeks and it was a huge relief to be told he was free. He relayed that good news to Daisy as the strolled through one of the parks in London, Jess was so happy she threw herself into his arms and he swung her round until she was dizzy.

"Marry me Daisy, marry me! I love you, I love you, I love you. I can't do this without you, my life has been empty away from you. Marry me tomorrow, we can have a big wedding later, just marry me." he was serious.

"Yes, yes, a thousand times yes! Of course I will marry you, I love you too. Oh my God I am so happy," she was smiling and laughing at the same time. She never expected him to ask her yet and certainly not out of the blue like that. It wasn't the most romantic proposal but heartfelt and natural. She was beaming.

"I want to take you home to meet my parents, they will love you and know how I feel about you, I have told them how kind and wonderful you have been, what do you think?" he hoped she would agree, and soon.

They were having dinner in their hotel and chatting about their lives and hopes for the future laughing and enjoying each other's company, when Daisy suddenly held up her menu in front of her face and said "Look who has just come in, Dom, what do we do? Don't look round, look at me, it's my father and the Russian and another man, I've never seen him before. I can't believe it, of all the places in this City, he comes into our hotel!"

Luckily for Daisy and Dominic the three men went to the bar and not into the restaurant enabling the couple to slip away and upstairs without being seen. Daisy was curious though and wanted to go back down to spy on her father. Dominic laughed when she said spy on her own father.

"That is ridiculous, why don't you just go and say hello?"

"Should I?" It was a simple question to a complicated situation between them.

"Do you know I might just do that! I wonder what he will say?

Would you stay up here while I go down? I don't think I want him to know you are here. We have never talked about you since... well you know since that last time? What do you think?" she was asking him with a heavy heart. The last thing she wanted was to hide him away, she wanted to show him off to the world, shout it from the rooftops, say I love him, and we are going to be married! But this was her father, her irrational, stupid father who had battered the love of her life. The last thing she wanted was a confrontation spoiling her wonderful day and her wonderful news.

"Of course, go! I don't want to meet him here, it might be difficult. Go and see if you can find out what he is doing here," he kissed her, turned her round and gave her a friendly push towards the door of the hotel bedroom. She blew him a kiss as she went through it and said she wouldn't be long.

The look on Alex's face when Daisy walked up to them in the bar was one of complete shock. He was deep in conversation with Nikolai, in Russian when she approached them. He had no chance to stop the conversation, it was too late, she had heard him. She knew she hadn't imagined it that first time at home.

"Daisy, Daisy! What a surprise, what are you doing here? Is Jess with you? Erm, Daisy, this is Nik and Johan, Nik, Johan this is Daisy my daughter," she was embarrassed. She had no idea why, but this was not the place to meet your father and two dodgy friends when you have a lover upstairs.

"Sit down, would you like a drink?" Alex asked.

"Yes, I will have a gin and tonic please, what are you doing here Dad?" her question was direct, and it was his turn to look embarrassed. Alex was in London with Nikolai finalising an arms deal with this South African Johan Drynmaar. But he was not going to tell her that. Johan looked equally embarrassed and slightly terrified at her arrival, she thought.

"What are you doing here?" he asked the same question.

"Oh just spying on my father," she enjoyed that quip, but it didn't go down too well. Alex stood up and took her arm, leading her away from the other two men and out into the reception area.

"What the hell was that supposed to mean? Spying on my father? Not funny Jess. What has happened to you? I am here on business and not what I want those two to hear, my daughter saying she is spying on me, joke or not."

"OOO tetchy, why are you speaking in Russian?" she was direct and wanted an answer.

"Because they speak Russian better than English and I need to know what they are offering me, it's my work Daisy! Now, can we meet tomorrow, I need to continue with these guys," he was sounding quite stroppy, and she pulled her arm away. She also thought he was lying.

"Jess is worried, she said she hasn't seen you for three days and no phone call. I will tell her I have seen you speaking Russian again!" She was feeling brave. "I saw you with him at home in the garden, Jess knows you met with him before," and we know who he is, 'the striped haired' bloke, from next door, he is living at The Copse, Jess knows him, and Maria knows you are meeting him. You need to tell her what is going on or I will," she turned and left him standing there open mouthed.

Two seconds later, she turned around again and strode back to where he was still standing, on the same spot, watching her leave.

"Oh and I am getting married. You won't be invited to the wedding, but I thought you needed to know," she grinned as she spoke and then turned her back on him and left him standing there for the second time. It felt like revenge, and she liked it, but the point scoring did not stop that single tear trickle down her face.

Glynis.M.Parkes

Chapter 27

"I know you remember Martin Squire," Devlin was about to give Maria some very good news but needed to build it up a bit just for effect. This was his moment, and he would savour the delivery of the news.

"Yes I remember Martin, your friend, very stylish…" she was very fond of Martin and would have been fonder if he had been a little bit more affectionate towards her, but it wasn't to be. "Loved his jewellery if I remember correctly, clever man, and smart clothes," she remembered him for his outlandish style. How could she forget those beautiful pale blue leather suits and expensive watches and rings.

"Why are you asking me about Martin Squire?"

"Well, as you say he loved his jewellery, we both did, he wore it - I stole it for him," there he said it. He had never told another soul in the world about that part of his life. Only Martin knew. Maria said nothing, she was lost for words for the first time in a long time. When she did speak she asked the obvious question.

"You stole jewellery?"

"You heard correctly, I stole jewellery, I was a burglar, a robber, a thief! Big time and we did well, all over Europe, Stately

Homes, big houses, museums, hotels, the best jewellery houses, we made a fortune," he smiled as he remembered.

"I don't understand? Why are you telling me this now?" She was at a loss, what was he saying?

"Well my darling new wife who wants a safe opening... how do you think we stole jewellery? Yes, she gets it!" He noticed the light go on in Maria's head. "We got it mainly from safe cracking and I am that man who can crack a safe," now he had more than a smile, it was a very smug look on his face.

"Oh...my...GOD..." she got up and poured two more large vodkas, drinking one as she stood by the bottle and filled her own glass up again. How did she not know this fact about him.

"No need for violence, just tell me when and I will be there, I will need an hour 'max, be nice if I am not under pressure but if I have to I can have it open in an hour."

"Leave it with me I will speak to Jess," she slurred after so much vodka, then hugged him, thinking he might be useful after all. They finished the bottle.

"Alex is away, he is in London and not back until tomorrow. He just rang me, weirdly, he ran into Daisy, and she reminded him to call me. I haven't seen him for four days," Jess told Maria when she rang at 8 am.

Maria sounded excited and said she and Devlin were coming round for breakfast if she was sure Alex was away and not due back. Sure enough, half an hour later there they both were on the doorstep practically jumping up and down trying to get into the house.

"What NOW? You are going to open it NOW?" Jess was stunned and felt sick and excited and a hundred emotions she could not explain.

"Put the kettle on and we can leave Dev to it…" Maria told Jess to go into the kitchen and she followed her, leaving Devlin in the living room with his bag of tools and a powerful torch. Jess asked no more questions and the two women made themselves scarce. Time for explanations.

Maria had no more idea of Devlin's past than Jess and when she had finished explaining they were now concerned that Alex might suddenly appear. Daisy had assured Jess that he was in London and told her he was not coming back today so she had to trust that information. She had no idea why he was in London, and it was now Jess's turn to explain what Daisy had discovered in the hotel over the past twenty four hours.

"What! Alex was with the Russian? I don't understand Jess. We knew Nikolai was up there with a South African contact, finalising a deal we have ongoing but to meet with Alex? What are they up to? I won't tell Devlin until he is finished. He will lose all concentration if he knows right now, let's not mention it. I will tell him when he has opened the safe. The phone rang in the hall and Jess got up to answer it. Maria heard her say, "Oh hi Daisy, are you ok?"

"Is somebody there with you Jess?" Alex was quick and realised why she was saying that.

"Yes, Maria is here, we are just having a bit of breakfast and a natter, women stuff," she laughed.

Alex would not return to the Old Mill House the next day or the one after that. He told Jess it was better if he stayed away for a while as he thought he might be in danger but to trust him. He was oblivious to the fact that Devlin was about to reveal what was in the safe he had hidden from her for ten years. She decided not to tell Maria that he had rung her. She had to trust what he was saying. Trust? She couldn't believe that thought was in her head. A man who had a secret safe in their home. What on earth is inside it? She hoped nothing and all this was for nothing. Please God let it be nothing.

The two women kept looking through the crack in the door, watching to see if they could see any progress on the safe, drinking multiple cups of coffee they were chatting nervously about what was going on in the room next to them. It was unbearable waiting.

Just before noon, they heard Devlin shouting, "Maria, Jess, come in, you can come in, wow!"

The safe was open, Jess felt sick.

Devlin had pulled out most of the contents and he was sitting on the floor surrounded by dozens of velvet bags, files and money. It was an unbelievable sight. It reminded Jess of Christmas when Daisy was young, and she sat with that look on her face, joy and wonder at what she was looking at. Parcels all wrapped in pretty paper, with the anticipation of the contents being magical and exciting. There was no pretty paper spread in front of the big safe. Just a lifetime of lies.

The two women joined Devlin on the floor and went to grab bags and the files, Devlin stopped them. "Stop, let's be methodical about this, some of it is very old, the paperwork, put that in a pile over there and the old money, its old currency before decimalisation, not much there. These bags, ok, one at a time - Jess have you got any trays? I have an idea what is in them, and we don't want to lose anything," being sensible in a sweet shop crossed Jess's mind.

She ran into the kitchen and came back with a pile of wooden trays, and they laid them on the floor. One by one Devlin poured the contents of the dark blue and black velvet bags onto the trays. The two women watched him, stunned, saying nothing. It was a sight Jess thought she would never see in her lifetime.

Devlin stopped at bag number five, they counted the bags and there were twenty three in there, all full of diamonds and emeralds, rubies and yellow stones that Dev said were diamonds. He let out a howl when bag number five uncovered its secrets…

"Oh my God, that's Martins ring. It was a white gold ring

with emeralds, a thick band made in the 1920s and distinctive Art Deco, it had their initials inside it M and D with a heart between the initials. The colour drained from his face.

"I can say Maria that most of this is mine." He rested his back on the panelling with his legs out in front of him and cried.

None of them knew what to say, it was such a shock to see all of this in front of them, sparkling in the sun it looked like a million stars twinkling. It was all making sense now, Maria spoke to Devlin, "How can it be yours? What do you mean?"

"Martin looked after all of it, and when he died it went with him, I never knew what he had done with it all, I recognise some of it, his ring, this watch, the bracelet, look it is engraved, M….D – Martin, Devlin.

"What? You and Martin were…?" she didn't finish the sentence and he didn't respond to the question. Maria had a wave of understanding wash over her. It made sense now why Martin wasn't interested in her. She had no clue, it had never occurred to her.

"But how did it end up in this safe? I don't understand, somebody tell me," Jess was asking the question, it didn't make sense to her.

"Matt! Matt and Martin met several times, he must have offered to keep it all in the strong boxes in the vault in the bank in Zurich. He knew it would be safe there. No wonder I couldn't find it, and I have searched over the years believe me.   We had a fortune then, when Martin died, suddenly I had nothing," Devlin explained

"But how did it get here?" Jess still had no clue.

"Well I told you Matt went to empty the boxes in Zurich and found them empty, he blamed me, thought I had the contents of the boxes. He assumed I had taken all the money and obviously this little lot. But it wasn't me. Jess I hate to tell you this, and I know you are not making the connection, but it was Alex who took it all," she watched Jess's face as the truth dawned on her.

"Alex? Alex stole the money and these diamonds from the strong boxes, but why?"

Maria knew exactly why, revenge for his wife's death in that damned car accident. Matt was driving and she was killed but didn't admit it. Bloody Matt.

"Well I think his first wife Suzy took all the details of the boxes and the bank accounts and gave all the information to Alex. I think she was having an affair with Matt, and he rejected her. She did it out of revenge. When she died Alex blamed Matt for her death and taking this lot was his revenge. Double revenge if you like. She left out her involvement in the explanation and Jess seemed to be accepting it was all Matt's fault.

"What do we do with all of this?" Devlin felt overwhelmed by the sight of it all. He and Maria both knew now where the two million in diamonds came from to pay the 'sweetener' to the Cartels. Alex was involved but why?

"Take it…take it all, I don't want any of it in the house. Let me look at those files though, I need to read them and see if there are any clues to Alex's life. Devlin had picked up one of them and was flipping through it, making puffing noises and lots of wow's and oh's.

"Wow Jess, he bought property all over the island, five apartments in Cowes, a farm in Carisbrook and houses in Chale, the man is a genius!" he laughed, a true criminal recognising another. "That is just one file. I will leave the rest for you to browse through," he was scooping up the diamonds and jewels back into the bags as he spoke to her. He put a handful of diamonds into a bag and gave them to Jess. She held up her hands and said, "No, I don't want them."

"Yes you do, take them, call it insurance, there must be a million there alone. You just never know when you might need it, you and Daisy," Devlin insisted.

Chapter 28

September 10th, 1979

"Daisy, could you come into the office please. I need your advice," Daisy's partner Elizabeth, was ringing her at home. There was something she needed Daisy to see before she made a phone call. So much had happened during the previous week while Daisy was in Mallorca with her new husband.

"Give me an hour, I have just got here, and I need to go and see Jess first to update her on what has happened in Mallorca, and for her to update me on what happened next door. I have called in to the apartment in Cowes to check everything is ok, so I won't be long."

Daisy had been in Mallorca for a week meeting Dom's parents, as the new Mrs Montpelier following a small ceremony in a register office in London with two strangers as witnesses. She felt like the happiest woman in the world, it was such a whirlwind of events and emotions, within twenty four hours of being married Dom whisked her off to Mallorca to meet his parents and introduce her to his sister and her family. She had not even seen Jess or her father since she had married Dom, there had been no time, but Jess encouraged her to go and have a wonderful time. She was overjoyed for Daisy.

She had only been in Mallorca for two days when suddenly out of the blue and without any previous history, his father had a heart attack and there was nothing they could do to save him. It was so sudden and such a shock. His mother was beside herself with grief one minute and not sure what was going on the next so Dom and his sister were speaking to a lovely nursing home that would take her straight away, her dementia had deteriorated rapidly over the last few months anyway and they wanted the best care for her. Daisy had only known his father for a couple of days, and she was as in love with him as anybody she had ever met in her life. In those two days, she fell under his charms and as quickly as she fell for Dom. What a character, he was so warm and welcoming, she was devastated.

When she arrived at the Castle on the hillside in Mallorca Daisy was stunned by the size and beauty of the house. It felt as if she had stepped into a dream. She had no idea about any of it. Dom had said nothing about his home or the scale and grandeur of it. It was a castle on the hillside, a CASTLE! She laughed when she saw it, it was just huge, with 40 odd rooms, 23 bedrooms, a huge library and ballroom, it even had armed guards at the gate! She had guessed he was from a good background by the way he behaved but this was like something out of a magazine, or a Bond Film set. There was so much to learn about Dom and his family background.

She travelled back to the Isle of Wight to see Jess who was struggling to decide what to do about Alex after the dramatic events of the previous weekend next door at The Copse, and things she had discovered in some paperwork a safe in the house. Daisy was dreading it and was worried about her. Her father and Jess were so in love it was embarrassing for Daisy sometimes, especially when she was growing up, but as she got older she XXXealized she wanted a relationship exactly like theirs. They had been so close, so strong, so in love, and now it seemed it had all crumbled.

September 2nd, 1979

Everything had gone to plan. If ever a phrase suited an occasion it was 'it went like clockwork,' fitted perfectly, to describe the weekend of the drugs and weapons drop in Chale Bay.

The two tankers arrived more or less on time, as they came around the Bay the men all cheered in silence when they saw them slide across the horizon in the moonlight, five minutes late after thousands of miles was nothing and their arrival helped alleviate the blood pressure levels in so many of the crew who were full of nervous energy waiting in the dark for the off-load to begin. The goods were taken off by the hyped up crew in super speed time mid channel and stashed in two caves. One was just not big enough for this massive haul. The distribution the next day went to plan when the second wave of small boats took it off all around Great Britain and off to France and Europe. The weapons were collected by a crew from Northern Ireland late on Sunday night, the last consignment to go. This was the most difficult to monitor with people on the beach in the sunshine that day, but they did it. Massive amounts of money went into bank accounts, hands were shaken, and the job was completed. Maria and Devlin were overjoyed and feeling smug.

"Jess I'm home," Daisy called out to her, and she appeared looking less than happy and certainly not her usual self. It was obvious she had not slept. After giving Daisy the biggest hug that went on for longer than was normal, Daisy looked at her, and was shocked at her appearance, she had lost weight and looked pale. Her unwashed hair was dragged back into an untidy ponytail that hung greasy and limp. It was so unusual for Jess to neglect her hair.

"I can tell you are not yourself Jess, but I am here to rescue you," she tried to be light hearted and upbeat but she felt it would take more than that to lift Jess right now.

"What is the point, Alex has gone, it is such a mess. How have we got to this after ten years?" she sounded so sad and so low.

"Jess tell me what has happened, it all sounds so awful," she needed to know all of it.

"No you first, I am so sorry about Dom's father and all of this Daisy, it should be the happiest time of your life and you are dealing with so much, you should be with him not me," she spoke with so much love and felt so little at that moment. She didn't want to be a nuisance right now and just wanted to be on her own if only she had the guts to say that to Daisy but didn't want to hurt her feelings.

"Don't be silly, Dom and his sister are sorting it all out, the funeral was very quick, it left no time to really think about it! They have already found a lovely nursing home for his Mum. His sister wants us to live in the house, she will stay at the farm. Their solicitor says the house will come to Dom anyway when his Mum dies, and they have left the farm to his sister so no complications there. They are better with me out of the way for a few days, the old lady is confused enough as it is, she had no idea who I am most of the time. Now what about you? What on earth has happened?

Jess started to cry, it was awful seeing her so unhappy, but she started to talk and some of it didn't make sense to Daisy, and she had to keep asking Jess to repeat things, just so she could get it clear in her head.

Glynis.M.Parkes

Chapter 29

"The b**stard has been in the safe! It's all gone! He left me a note, a bloody note," Alex was beside himself with anger, he smashed his fist on the table and Jess came into the kitchen to see what all the noise was. He was speaking to Nikolai on the phone and looked up at her with a glare that scared her and said, 'get out of here.' She had never heard him so angry. He waited while she left the room before continuing his conversation and her instincts told her to make herself scarce, so she left the house and went for a walk up into the woods.

"That Devlin Marshall has emptied the f*...g safe! I know it was him because he left a note...what do you mean what did it say? It said I have emptied the f*...g safe! Words to that effect. It actually said and I quote 'sweet revenge, thank you for keeping it safe for us - Martin & Devlin,' He has our diamonds, the family diamonds. Well he won't get away with it, meet me in an hour, bring the rifles." He was fuming, all those years he had thought the family diamonds were safe, diamonds that Devlin Marshall and Martin Squire stole from his family, the Markarov's in Russia, stolen from their business and left them with nothing. He wanted them back, Nikolai wanted his family back, they wanted the family honour back. A family reduced to poverty after decades of hard work that had made them money and given them status in Moscow. All reduced to nothing and handouts, because of Marshall and Squire.

Matt Hayward had placed the diamonds into his vault in Zurich as a favour to Martin Squire all those years ago. For a very large fee Alex had paid Matt to do it, thinking Matt would give them back to Alex but he refused. They had a big fight about it here, outside the Old Mill House. Jess saw them fighting and he had made up some excuse of mistaken identity, but he knew Matt very well. He would take money to do anything and was paid by MI5 and MI6 to do some deals and give up names. This time his own greed got the better of him and he put the gems into his own vault in the bank in Zurich.

Alex got them back with the help of information from his first wife Suzy, hiding them away in a safe in his own house, for more than ten years, and now he had lost them again – to the very man who stole them in the first place. It was an evil circle of crime, led by ingenuity from Suzy, the circumstance of her job with Matt and Maria, luck that Maria fleetingly saw the safe, and greed from all of them. Alex was livid but would not let this one lie. He wasn't finished with Devlin Marshall and that bloody woman next door. Oh no.

Alex had no idea if Jess knew what had happened here, but he mulled it over and over in his head and kept coming back to the conclusion, she knew nothing about the safe and its contents. How could she possibly know?

Maria put the ice into the glass and handed it to Devlin, who was standing like a King overlooking his domain, he leaned on the rail of the glass balcony feeling triumphant at the magnitude of what they had just pulled off in Chale Bay.

"Well here's to you and me and the future," he raised his glass and Maria looked at him and chinked her glass against his.

"I think we should go away for a while… let the dust settle, what do you think? On your boat maybe or a cruise. I could see myself sitting on the deck of a massive cruise ship with a glass in one hand and a book in the other, or we could trade in yours and buy a bigger yacht," Maria was dreaming of her elegant future, with or without Devlin. She still had not made up her mind what to do about him.

"A book? You? Reading a book!" he laughed and went to fill his glass up again. But he got no further than turning away from the glorious view, when Maria fell to the ground, a single shot rang out and she was on the floor, lying on the glass that was quickly turning red. He looked at her and stepped back from the front of the balcony, away from danger. He lifted his glass as he watched her lying there, dying in front of him.

"Oh my sweet, what have they done to you? Thank you for the ride, thank you for all of this," he waved his glass around the room as if taking it all in. He was gloating at the joy of seeing her lying there bleeding to death, his mind racing ahead with so many thoughts, they had got her, they had finally got her, and he would be free, free to enjoy all of this.

Maria was gasping for air, the bullet had gone through her lung, and she was bleeding out profusely, her voice was just a whisper as she tried to breathe and stay alive.

"Do something you moron, ring for help," she was pleading with him.

"Devlin…help me," she wheezed and gasped for breath.

"I can't hear you," he mocked, unmoved by seeing her laying there, he felt nothing.

"Don't let me die," she laughed

"Only you could laugh," he leaned over her to make sure she could hear him.

"Die you old hag, I hate you, I have always hated you. But thank you for making my life so much easier, I will enjoy all of this, the money, the house, all of it, cheers," and he raised his glass over her.

Her voice was just a whisper, and she asked him again to help her,

"Get help Devlin, if I die you get nothing… do you think I would leave this house to you? You are a bigger fool than I thought. You get nothing when I die, I only ever had one friend and she gets the lot, " she thought of Jess as she smiled her last smile.

He straightened himself up, standing over her in disbelief at her final words, he pushed her body with his foot, "Wake up you vile woman, wake up, what do you mean, she gets the lot?" But he knew it was too late.

Another shot rang out and hit him right between his eyes. Theo was a crack shot, and he was doing this for the Markarov family honour, his family. Devlin was dead before he hit the glass floor of his beloved glass balcony that was now dripping with Maria's blood. He fell on top of her, and his blood ran like a river into hers and dripped over the edge of the balcony.

The Copse was empty, Jamal had left, gone back to Paris to enjoy the peace and freedom the new money would afford him and his family.

Nikolai, Theo and Alex, put the rifles into the carrying bags and strolled up to the house. They were determined to ransack The Copse until they found the missing diamonds and gems. Theo, Nikolai's son, finally being able to shake off the deception that he was related to Jamal. They had just assumed, but it was useful for him to be able to listen and relay information, without being exposed as the Russians son. They trusted Jamal and so to bring him in as his son seemed like the best plan, and it worked, nobody questioned it. But the irony was that there was nobody left who would care… Nikolai fulfilled his promise to the Cartel he would avenge the woman who took their money. The second part of the agreement he made, 2 million in diamonds and the life of Maria Hayward. Job complete.

They found the pile of velvet bags stuffed with gems, hidden in the panic room. There was no safe it was all just there on a shelf waiting to be taken back. Alex went back to the Old Mill House and told Jess what had happened. He explained there were some people looking for Maria and Devlin who had been involved in the Chale Bay drugs Organisation and Jess accepted it.

She knew she would have to get away from there now, there had been too many secrets and too much hidden from her over the last ten years. Too much sorrow, too many deaths. Alex was still estranged from Daisy which was ridiculous and this safe business and all the things he had done over the years without her knowledge were eating into her. The paperwork she found exposing him as a fraud, not the man she married. New identities, property he bought without her knowing, money he had laundered. His secret Russian family, he left her out of all of that and she wanted no part of it now. She felt it was over, it had to be over. Her heart was broken.

True to her word Maria bequeathed everything to Jess in her will. If Devlin outlived her he got nothing. Jess was mortified and shocked when she heard but wanted no part of The Copse, it had been nothing but bad luck and trouble for her and Maria over the years. She would sell it and give it all to charity. The least she could do.

Chapter 30

1985 Mallorca

"Could I please speak to Mrs Montpelier,"

"Sorry Sir Mrs is dead, a couple of years now," Alex just muttered, 'Daisy dead?' He was shocked and took a step backwards, trying not to fall over, his knees suddenly giving way under him, he grabbed the railing to steady himself.

He was at the gates of The Castle in Mallorca, he had not been there for nearly six years, since he visited Dom's parents to tell them he was alive and in England. It looked the same, the guards looked the same, but he felt very different. His life was now so different to what it was back then. He had not been invited but he missed Jess and Daisy, his only family apart from Nikolai, who had moved to Switzerland with his own family and made no contact now.

"Mrs McFarlane is home, would you like to speak to her?" Alex nodded as the guard enquired and picked up the telephone to summon someone from the house to escort Alex in to see his wife. A wife he had not seen for some years now, God he missed her, his stomach was in knots at the very thought of seeing his Jess again.

How could he deal with this, the third bit of devastating news in his life, Jess leaving him, the safe being emptied and now Daisy is dead, it was too much to bear.

Jess looked up as the maid brought Alex out onto the balcony, she smiled at him. It had been a long time.

She was sitting on the balcony with children around her. Thomas who was four, was on the floor playing with his bricks, building a tall tower then knocking it down again and again. Baby Hannah who was nearly one, was on her lap and jumping up and down stretching her legs. Alex had not seen them before and as he sat beside Jess he held the baby's tiny hand in his.

"Jess," he didn't know what to say to her, it had been nearly six years of emptiness. He tried in the beginning to make contact, but it was useless, so he stopped and let her be. A few days ago somebody from the staff here got in touch to tell him that Jess had cancer and only had months to live. He jumped on the first flight.

" Daisy? What happened to Daisy?" He was in tears, how could he cope with this? "I am so sorry Jess, I should have come before and made it all up with her, and now it's too late."

"What do you mean?" she was puzzled by his question.

"The guard on the gate said she was dead," he sniffed.

"No, the old lady, Mrs Montpelier senior is dead, his English isn't that good, my God Alex what a shock for you. Sorry, no Daisy is fine, she will be back soon, she will be so pleased to see you."

He put his arm around her, and she rested her head on his shoulder. A tear trickled down her face and fell onto his arm.

"Stay," she whispered.

"I am not going anywhere," he knew he would hold her close for the rest of the life she had left.

Printed in Great Britain
by Amazon

24404560R00145